Compulsive

A Novel by

JACK ENGELHARD

DayRay Literary Press
British Columbia, Canada

Compulsive: A Novel

Copyright ©2013 by Jack Engelhard
ISBN-13 978-1-77143-081-4
First Edition

Library and Archives Canada Cataloguing in Publication
Engelhard, Jack, 1940-, author
Compulsive: a novel / by Jack Engelhard. – First edition.
Issued in print and electronic formats.
ISBN 978-1-77143-081-4 (pbk.).--ISBN 978-1-77143-082-1 (pdf)
Additional cataloguing data available from Library and Archives Canada

Compulsive: A Novel by Jack Engelhard has been registered with the
United States Copyright Office.

Jack Engelhard may be contacted through: **www.jackengelhard.com**

Cover artwork: Red dice rolling on green felt.
Picture © Michele Galli | iStockphoto.com
Author photo on back cover © Christopher Johnson.

DayRay Literary Press is a literary imprint
of CCB Publishing: www.ccbpublishing.com

DayRay Literary Press
British Columbia, Canada
www.dayraypress.com

International Bestselling Novelist Jack Engelhard
Author of _Indecent Proposal_

Translated into more than 22 languages and turned into a Paramount motion picture of the same name starring Robert Redford and Demi Moore.

Compulsive is a journey through today, with issues as current as the morning paper, brought to the fore by characters as timeless as the Bible. All this processed through a mind addicted to gambling as surely as others are addicted to heroin. A brisk read by one of America's most accomplished authors... not to be missed. Jack Engelhard, the last of the Hemingways, is a writer without peer and the conscience of us all.

Laurels from author of _J.D. Salinger: A Life_
for Engelhard's novel _Compulsive:_

"_Compulsive_ is enormously enjoyable, and so easy to get into. That Jack Engelhard is a talented novelist is self-evident. His story plots are engrossing, his writing is fluid, and his characters are easily recognizable. They are as flawed and complex as flesh and blood people. And like actual people, they are often confronted by moral choices. This is where Jack Engelhard becomes an important novelist. By presenting his characters with moral roadblocks, the author asks us, as readers, to examine our own ethics. That's rare in today's literature. In an age where moral ambiguity has become a staple of fashionable writing, Jack Engelhard pulls us back to remind us that our lives are a consequence of the ethical decisions we make."

- Kenneth Slawenski, (Random House) bestselling author of _J.D. Salinger: A Life_ - www.deadcaulfields.com

<u>Additional praise received for *Compulsive*:</u>

"*Compulsive* takes you inside the mind of a compulsive gambler. It is not an external narrative or a journalistic account. It is written as such a person *thinks*. It jumps from one adventure, one issue, one moral conflict to another.... with no regard for the niceties of full resolution, tied up loose ends, completeness. Through it all we see the masterful orchestration of action that is pure Engelhard."
- John W. Cassell, author of *Crossroads: 1969*

"Jack Engelhard's new novel, *Compulsive*, features an articulate gambler/filmmaker who faces one emotional challenge after another. The dialogue is as real as Hemingway's, crisp and to the point. Engelhard's writing here has a raucous edginess that is fresh, original and superb in drawing us into the mind of a compulsive gambler. As with his earlier novels, especially the blockbuster *Indecent Proposal*, the central figure's moral dilemmas in *Compulsive* are the stuff we should all care about. The suspense is riveting. Engelhard, as always, masters economy of style. The novel ends with the hint of more to come--another book! In this one, Engelhard brings it home, again."
- Lois Sack, author of *Her Brightness in the Darkness*

"In *Compulsive* there are stories interwoven inside stories that keep the reading crisp and compelling until the end. Like the main character, Gil Gilels, it is easy to become "compulsive" to read more by Jack Engelhard. He is a master at creating moral dilemmas that make the reader think long after you finish reading the story."
- Bonnie Kaye, M.Ed., Counselor and author of
ManReaders: A Woman's Guide to Dysfunctional Men

Also by Jack Engelhard

Indecent Proposal: Fiction.
Translated into more than 22 languages and turned into a Paramount motion picture of the same name starring Robert Redford and Demi Moore.

Escape From Mount Moriah: Memoir.
Award-winner for writing and film.

Slot Attendant: *A Novel about a Novelist*. Fiction.

The Girls of Cincinnati: Fiction.

The Prince of Dice: Fiction.

The Bathsheba Deadline: Fiction.

The Horsemen: Non-fiction.

The Days of the Bitter End: Fiction.

Dedicated to
Leslie, David, Rachel, Sarah, Toni...and Siena!

Immeasurable gratitude to
Jeffrey Farkas, John W. Cassell, Linda Shelnutt

Chapter 1

A tap on the shoulder is never a good sign.

"Mr. G," said the man.

I was overextended on my credit, so it figured, but I was having a good run, finally. I had the boys around the table hollering at each toss of the dice.

"We got us a shooter!" said the stickman, accompanied by backslapping hoots and cheers.

So I was making the points. Good action. Bad timing.

"I'm in the middle of a shoot," I said, "and you can call me Gil. You know who I am."

Yes he did, and I knew who he was. I'd had this before from Zack Charles. He was part of Credit Security and maybe part of the Casino Control Commission as well here in Atlantic City. Every casino had one like him, only Zack was more zealous at his job than most, and he seldom approached on tiptoes. He pounced on his quarry. He was an intelligent man. There was no fooling him.

But I wasn't in the mood for this and neither were the boys who kept shouting at him to leave me alone.

"Let the guy shoot!"

"Mr. Gilels," said Zack, "please."

I'd ignore him as long as I could. I needed to make my point, which was the number six. I had developed a bad habit of depending on particular numbers. I had those same numbers even for the horses, occasionally, when the handicapping itself wasn't doing me much good. I had started to depend on pure luck, and more than that, on mysticism. That was never smart, to depend wholly on luck, when it was skill that separated the winners from the losers.

But the power of numerology also had to be believed. I knew people who spoke in numbers.

Crazy, but it was the mathematicians who reached out to *meaning* and *infinity* much more than the philosophers.

"Let's go," said Zack.

"You are interrupting my game," I said.

I was tipsy from the vodka. I seldom drank. But it had been a bad day, a bad week, a bad month, a bad year and there was sure to be more trouble ahead.

Dear God. There is trouble ahead.

"Please don't do that," I said when he tapped me again.

"We need to talk," he said.

You never want to hear that from the House.

"I got it going," I said.

Zack signaled for the stickman to remove the dice from my spot.

"New shooter," said the stickman.

"You can't do this," I said.

"Yes we can," said Zack. "Let's go for a walk."

That meant his office.

"What about my chips?"

"They'll be returned to you," said Zack.

Maybe they would. Maybe they wouldn't.

We started to walk across the casino floor, which was crowded and feverishly noisy as always. Was that me staggering? I had only had one drink, maybe two, but I was no drinker. That was not my vice. No, that one, that vice, they could not pin on me. I did smoke, so that was another flaw this new and improved world had against me. For some reason, I seemed to be on the outs with this new generation coming up.

I had picked this table because it was the only one that still permitted smoking. Drinking was permitted everywhere. I would never understand this.

My old man – old age has got him in a Home where smoking is forbidden but he cannot go to the bathroom without a cigarette.

A man bumped into me and he stopped and glared at me. He wanted trouble.

I let it go. You had to be careful. You never knew what kind of a day a man was having.

Road rage was everywhere.

"What's this all about?" I asked when we got to Zack's office.

He'd be in no rush. That's how they got you to worry, not knowing how deep you were in. They wanted you to sweat. They had it all worked out, the psychology of it all, where they got you tracing back to your misdeeds of not only today, but any day, and never mind the casino. Where else had you sidestepped or broken the law? What other sins had you committed?

The *eye in the sky* was atop every life and there was no hiding from gossips, snitches and talebearers.

"You can't keep playing over your head," he finally said.

He meant the tables. The horses were a different story. Over at the racing parlor you were mostly on your own, and that's where I did most of my business anyway.

"We can't let you keep doing this," he said.

If the casino was a mirror of life, it was this: You were not supposed to win. If you did, something was wrong.

"Why stop me when I was catching up?"

"Craps is not your game," he said. "So why bother?"

I bothered because I'd been in a bit of a slump with the horses and anyway, wasn't this a free country?

Not always.

"The State," he said, "is on our back. The State is concerned that we're enticing compulsive gamblers, and Gil, it's not like you're anonymous. Understand? You've got a name and once a month you're on Page Six if not all over the Internet – and they notice, believe me they do, and next thing you know they want answers, the State and the Commission."

"Did you say compulsive?" I asked.

He squirmed. He was really not a bad guy, like the guy with no neck in the racing room. Zack was only doing his job.

"Gil, you may not be compulsive..."

"Thank you..."

"But you do have the habit."

Now with the lottery in practically every state, I figured the entire nation to be compulsive.

"So I'm being iced?"

"Only from the tables, and only for a short time, until we get the authorities off our backs."

Maybe it was the State and the Commission that wanted me chilled, but I had other enemies that were even more authoritative and even more dangerous and who were angling to get a slice of me. I named them right here to myself and I got a case of the willies just thinking of them and of one man in particular. Payday was coming. I was short of means and that man was growing short of patience.

"Besides," said Zack. "Your dice toss has been noticed."

Aha.

"Noticed?"

"You know what I mean."

"I am not so sure," I said.

"Gil, let's just say that you have certain skills."

"I wish that were true."

"You win when you need to win."

"So how come I lose?"

"You lose when you need to lose."

They were suspicious that I was spinning the helicopter. Well, I did have a knack for hitting my points and for getting the ivories to sail out exactly where I wanted them to sail and land. Out in Vegas Slim Sam Belmont and Julian Rothschild had taught me some tricks. Quite legal if you didn't get caught, and quite successful if you didn't resort to the gimmick too often.

Julian, even more than Slim Sam, was positively messianic about gambling. Craps was his faith and his religion and he hated to be called a *mechanic*, and he hated it even more to be called compulsive. Every casino in town – there in Vegas – was after Julian's blood for breaking the rules, that is, he kept on winning. He gave half his winnings to charity.

So he taught me the helicopter, and he also taught me to be charitable with my wins.

The angels are always voting and you want them on your side. You want them voting in your favor.

Some of his mysticism rubbed off on me and he almost got me to believe that among the angels it always came down to one vote. Not much of a margin for error.

Julian was a mystic all right; not religious, but mystical. Big difference. He'd bring up Biblical Abraham and talk about the bargaining Abraham had to do to persuade God not to destroy the sinful cities of Sodom and Gomorrah...will You destroy the good together with the bad...the righteous together with the evil...and what if You find fifty good men in those places...and if not fifty then twenty...and if not twenty then five; "And in the end there weren't even five, and God destroyed them both, Sodom and Gomorrah."

The bargaining continues, for the entire world. This time it's in the hands of the 36 Just Men – and the voting starts anew from morning to morning.

That's how tenuously we exist.

Julian was still after me to get my act together for a documentary that was to follow the Israelites on their near 40-year wanderings in the desert from slavery to the Promised Land. He knew all the 42 stops they had made en route from Egypt. He knew his Bible. He even knew much of it by heart. He was serious about this and offered himself as a volunteer technical advisor, and I started to get serious about this myself. Could it be proven, this Biblical episode that so many believed and so many doubted?

Zack was still talking. I was only half listening.

"So give it a rest," Zack was saying.

There was no sense arguing.

"Go back to the horses."

Sure. What the hell?

So I went over to the horses, but, for some reason, I didn't feel much like playing. Rare for me, but I hadn't done much handicapping overnight. I usually spent two hours on the handicapping, which ordinarily qualified me as a horseracing degenerate, but I had it down to a science, and horseracing was my address. That's where anybody could find me when I wasn't working on my films and it's true, too often I was not working on my films.

The racing room was not the most attractive place in the world. Most of it was populated by angry old men. This was not the sport of kings the way it used to be when 40,000 fans gravitated to the big-time tracks even on weekdays. The stands were mostly empty and nowadays we did our wagering from the inside and watched our winners and losers from TV monitors.

I was about to leave when there was shouting over by the windows and that had to be the supervisor with no neck being his usual obnoxious self. He had as his prey Josh Beacon, the Pulitzer Prize winning playwright, of all people. Josh was an occasional horseplayer, not compulsive, *like some people*, but he was here often enough. The argument was about his lack of identification.

He'd won a taxable trifecta. This required three documents of identification. He only had two.

"You need three," said No Neck.

"I'm giving you my driver's license and a credit card," said Josh. "That's all I've got at the moment."

"Three," said No Neck. "Rules and regulations."

No Neck went strictly by the letter of the law, which usually meant his own laws. I once asked him for *a piece of paper* to write something down and he refused.

Now it was time for Josh to pull his ace in the hole.

"I have won a Pulitzer Prize," Josh said, pleadingly but firmly.

"What the fuck is that?" said No Neck.

I went over.

"What do *you* want?"

"Honest," I said. "This man won the Pulitzer Prize."

"I don't know what the fuck that is and I don't give a shit."

"You can look it up," I said.

7

"Look what up?"

"You can't be serious," said Josh. "You honestly never heard of the Pulitzer Prize."

"Nobody knows what that is," said No Neck.

"Nobody around here, that's for sure," Josh and I whispered together.

Josh and I looked around the room for further support. Smiley the Mooch was seated at one of the tables rooting in a horse. After the horse lost, as usual, I went over and asked him if he'd please help us out as he was practically the only degenerate in the joint that got along with No Neck, for some reason. Smiley had lived in LA and swore that he once dated Kim Novak. Anyway, he got around.

So Smiley the Mooch cooperated. He used the words that I had hastily taught him; confirming that Josh was true, blue Pulitzer.

"Yeah," he told No Neck. "It's legit."

"What is this Pulitzer?" No Neck asked Smiley.

"Beats me, but I think it's something like a bowling trophy, or golf."

No Neck said, "I bowl and I golf and I never heard of this prize."

"It's a regional thing," said Smiley, giving us a knowing wink. "Right?"

"Right," I said.

"Right," said Josh.

"Bowling?" No Neck asked Josh.

"Yes, bowling."

"Should have said so in the first place."

"You can look it up."

"I never look anything up."

"You'd find out what it really is."

"Bowling is good enough for me," said No Neck.

I was on my way out when I spotted Pastor Reickart without his collar. He never wore it at the track and he never tried to hide himself from anyone (though maybe from God Almighty). We exchanged awkward nods. No problem. He would make no judgments about me and I would make no judgments about him. He was tops as a handicapper and even entered the tournaments, which he often won. I suspected that this particular weakness must have begun not when he gave his Sunday sermons, but when he called Friday night Bingo. The allure of the devil was too much to resist, obviously. But I thought no less of him as a preacher when I saw him in church, and even when he spoke out so vigorously against Satan and the entrapments set by the devil. That was one place and this was another place. There he was one man and here he was another man.

I placed a few bets even though I had a plane to catch. I bet the numbers I had chosen for myself back then. Once in a while those numbers came in. Then I went over to the coffee shop that was situated right in the center of the casino, amid all the swarming action, and I sat there thinking, contemplating, lost in some sort of reverie, which never did me much good. Pessimism was my default position and what a commentary it was to realize that pessimists were right on target most of the time, far more often than optimists. We got it right 94.6 percent of the time, as I had it reckoned.

The place was hopping and I snapped to for some reason, to make myself aware that in fact, for all the buzz, I never saw the people. From end to end it was all a blur. I had seen all these people before so that it made no difference; it was all the same. Margie, the waitress, asked me if the soup was too hot or too cold. "Why?" I asked. "Because you're not eating."

So I ate and she came over again and wondered why I was laughing. People had begun to stare. Well I found myself hysterical about Josh Beacon. About the same time that he got the news and the congratulations from Columbia over his Pulitzer – just about then, maybe the same day, his latest play bombed on Broadway. The critics were scathing and it was about the only time that *The New York Times* and the *New York Post* agreed on anything.

Life in the big city or any city.

Chapter 2

I had to go to Montreal to pick up an award to be handed me for the documentary I did on Maurice "Rocket" Richard. For some reason I had trouble at the border. My papers weren't in order, or maybe it was my driver's license that had expired. I kept forgetting to get it updated as many times as I was stopped for this crime – and now I was being stopped again and seriously questioned. They even took me into a room for further interrogation and to prove I was who I said I was, Gil Gilels, filmmaker.

I showed them the fancy paperwork for the award and this made it worse because the *Legion of Documentary Film* people had misspelled my name. Finally I was let go and I registered at the Queen Elizabeth hotel and next day left my car there and took a cab to Schwartz's Deli on St. Laurent Boulevard for some of that world famous smoked meat. I had the whole day to kill. Festivities didn't start till 8. I was being honored along with four others. It was suggested that I wear a tux. No jeans, aye?

Well if it wasn't Andre who walked in.

"Motherfucker," he said.

"Son of a bitch," I said.

We kept saying that for a while.

We exchanged further pleasantries by exchanging silly punches – and Andre could hit! He was a giant, six feet, five inches, and he didn't speak. He roared. He called himself Black Dude and he could call himself whatever he wanted. He was a former New York City cop, but he had family in Montreal, as did I. We became pals by chasing the horses around the same New York racetracks. He was hard to miss because when he had a horse rounding the final turn everybody heard about it loud and clear. He had a knack for spotting the winner as soon as they left the gate.

He ordered two sandwiches and ate them both slowly and deliciously. He loved life. We talked horses for a while, and women.

"Horses and women," he said. "What else is there, man?"

He'd been married four times and could not remember the names of any of his wives. He had two sons and he did not know where they were.

"I'm a gambler," he said. "That's what I am."

He had warned his sons never to introduce him to their girls "because I'm after the same tail, understand?"

I told him what I was doing in town.

"You did that?" he said, when I mentioned Richard. "I saw that movie, HBO or something."

"Or something."

"You big time now?"

"Canada thinks so."

"Can I come?"

"Who's to stop you," I said and we both laughed because it was the truth. Nobody stopped Black Dude Andre.

"I can prove to you that I saw your flick," he said, after I told him that everybody says that about a film of yours that they never saw. "You ready?"

"I'm ready."

"More career goals than assists and that never happens in hockey or in any sport. Fire on ice, that man."

I helped him out with the exact statistics: 544 career goals compared to 421 assists.

"So now they're honoring you for that, a horse degenerate like you?"

I never much cared for awards, mostly when they went to other people. Anyway, we do the best we can and sometimes it falls into place.

He was back in Montreal to meet up with a woman.

"We don't have enough women in the United States?" I said.

"Not like this one."

Her name was Suzanne (and there'd been others for him with the same name) and he described in some detail her legendary skills in bed.

"She has a sister, you know."

"Maybe some other time," I said.

"You and Barbara still split?"

"Yes," I said. "Yes, yes, yes."

"How could she do what she did?"

"Well she did."

"Sorry to bring it up, pal. But I know she broke your heart."

I was surprised that he knew. Had I told him? Or was this something that everyone knew?

"Is there a chance?" he asked about us ever getting back.

"The investigation continues."

"Hah!"

We knew that line well. He knew it from being a cop and I knew it from covering the police beat at the *Burlington County Times* – and it became my motto.

The investigation continues.

That was true not only for police work, but it was the theme for the big picture, life in general. Nothing in life was tidied up neatly. Nothing in life was ever resolved.

The investigation continues.

This Suzanne – there was one other detail.

"She's married, you know."

"Aren't they all?"

"But a man's got to do what a man's got to do."

He's got to go to the races, that's for sure, but Blue Bonnets had shut down so that, remarkably and tragically, there was no live horseracing in Montreal.

"How can people live like that?" I said.

"Beats me," he said.

But there was a casino – the Casino de Montreal.

"What time are you meeting this Suzanne," I asked, "and how can you tell one Suzanne from another?"

"Not till later," he said, "and I can't."

"What do you think?" I said.

"Don't you have to get ready? You got a big day coming."

"Plenty of time."

We got a cab and simply said, "Casino."

"Can't get that wrong in French or in English," I whispered to Andre.

"Yeah, the language police."

The cabbie said something in French and it wasn't nice.

"You still want a separate country?" Andre asked the cabbie – Andre simply looking for trouble.

The cabbie said something else in French and it still wasn't nice.

"He could throw us out," Andre said.

"Let him try," I said.

Tension was still in the air in Montreal and all over Quebec over a remark made by Charles de Gaulle back here in 1967 – *Vive Quebec Libre*; "Long Live Free Quebec." For centuries there'd been tensions between the French and the English about who really owned this land, the province of Quebec specifically, until finally the French got the upper hand. All signs had to be in French only, including, if possible, the red, yellow and green traffic signals. If English, in some cases, was grandfathered in, it had to be discreet and dominated loudly by French signage.

Maurice Richard, French-Canadian down to his toes, got tangled up in this, but he refused to take sides. He only wanted to "shoot da puck."

That's what he said when he was asked how it was that he scored so many goals.

"I shoot da puck," he said.

I did not know why we were going to the casino except that this was what we did, for the money, for the kicks, for the thrill.

"He's taking us for a ride," Andre said, then to the driver: "Hey, how many times you taking us around the city?"

The cabbie responded in French, but talking mostly to himself.

I made out this much: something about rude Americans.

"We're getting out," I said.

"Stop right here," ordered Andre.

But the man kept driving, and we were into some bad neighborhoods. When he stopped for a light, we got out, paid him, and this time in English:

"Not enough," he said.

"That's what the fucking meter says," Andre said.

15

"Tip," said the man.

"No tip," I said.

"Tip," said the man.

"We'll call the cops," said Andre.

Now some pushing and shoving and this was not the first time when I'd had to separate Andre from his prey.

So instead the son of a bitch called the cops and they were upon us in three minutes. This cop explained to us in English that the cabbie was in the right.

"Just pay him."

"We did."

"His cab. His rules."

I explained that this was not how it worked in the United States (though I wasn't sure if I had the facts exactly straight about the rules of tipping).

"This is not the United States," said the cop, English-speaking but with a French-Canadian accent. "You people think we are part of your neighborhood?"

Yes, that's what we thought.

"Canada is a sovereign nation, a foreign country to you."

We keep forgetting that part.

Yes, Canada is a foreign country. We still dominate their culture, but they have their own laws.

So we paid the tip. Andre was still grumbling about this even when we caught another cab, this time with a friendlier cabbie, fresh from Greece.

He spoke no English and no French. But soon enough he would learn his French.

A madhouse this casino, and equal to the glamour of anything we had back home.

"Knock 'em dead," said Andre and we separated to different tables for the games of dice.

I had a hot shooter who kept nailing his points. I was flush with black chips until he sevened-out, and when the dice were passed, I decided to move on. Seldom did it happen that you had two hot shooters in a row and besides, this guy's wife or girlfriend stepped up to the table to share her joys from the slot machines – and that was always bad luck.

Never tell your woman how much you won, was Andre's motto. They'll want all your winnings and then some for new carpets and curtains.

Well, sometimes true, but I sometimes brought Barbara along, and she was a trouper. She was a trouper all right.

I heard a commotion at some other table and I knew right away who it had to be. Andre was killing them.

"You want an eight. I'll give you an eight. Here's a comes an eight!" Sure enough, he made his point – and kept making them, each time accompanied by public announcements. He was on a roll. The table got crowded. The boys were always on the lookout for action like this. They patrolled the floors for the man with the hot hand.

I joined in and played whatever he played, and started stacking up. Andre's eyes stayed glued to the table. He did not survey his neighbors, fearing the distraction. Everything depended on staying in rhythm, and the dealers knew this, so once in a while they tried to disrupt him by taking their time making change or calling the cage for a fresh supply of chips, when none was necessary.

Andre finally caught the bad seven. The players, the boys, kept passing the dice. They refused to take their turns, hoping the dice would get back to Andre.

The pit boss announced that this was against the rules.

The dice landed on me, and now I got it going. I did better than Andre, who kept shouting, "That's my boy."

Finally I hit the cursed seven. We got ourselves to the casino restaurant. Andre never drank, period. I never drank when we gambled. But we were drunk – drunk on the action, drunk on our winnings. We checked the time and there was still time for our real business though in fact wasn't it this – wasn't this our real business? Andre already had something going with one of the waitresses, though her name wasn't Suzanne, it was Suzette.

"Is this the life!" Andre said.

Sure thing, only I was starting to worry about making it on time for the festivities on my behalf. I could not miss an event like that, so many people dependent on me, but so were the tables, and so we went back, and this time the casino got even, and we ended up near broke. "This never happened to me before," Andre said. "Me neither," I said. We blamed it on the language barrier. But we were tapped out.

Neither of us would dare approach an ATM. That would be sick and prove yourself to be a certifiable degenerate. No, this we would not do.

Actually, I would, but not around Andre. His gambling was under control.

We had enough cash for a cab, and of course we had our credit cards, so we went outside where all the cabs were taken except for one, and as if our luck hadn't turned lopsided enough, it was cab driver number one. Had he been waiting for us? We stepped in without a word, gave him our destinations and we took off for parts unknown.

"Where are you taking us?" asked Andre.

For me, it was getting close to six o'clock. I still needed to shower and shave and change clothes, and relax.

Gambling took its toll. In fact I was still sweating and my heart was still pounding from all the gambling, and I was still regretting all the wrong moves I had made – and, most of all, why hadn't I quit while I was ahead? Why this need to break the bank and take the House all the time?

Andre already had apologies to make with Suzanne.

"Where are you taking us?"

The cabbie answered in French.

He dropped us off on Clark Street. This was nowhere near where we had to go.

Neither of us wanted another argument or to have him call the cops on us again, but he did when we didn't have enough cash.

He refused to take American credit cards.

One cop arrived.

"No money?" he said.

We explained.

He managed to get the cabbie to accept my credit card, but he gave us a summons. We'd have to appear in court...at some later date.

Andre got on the phone and rented us a car and I was back at the hotel by 7:55. I'd never make it to the banquet on time, and not in this shape. I'd have to explain this somehow. More difficult was how I was to explain this to myself. Again, I had let people down, thanks to the gambling. I did not know where this came from, this urge, this craving.

Chapter 3

Again there were difficulties at the border. I was responsible for an outstanding summons. But I was let go.

For some reason my papers were never in order for
Canada, our neighbor to the north. That was part of a big
story. My mom had conceived me in Canada. My dad had
been invited to Montreal to give a talk related to his latest bestseller, and Mom would never let him go anywhere
alone and he would never go anywhere without Mom
anyway.

She was into her ninth month with me, but she accompanied him regardless. Somehow, on the train back, I
decided to get born. My mom tried to reach the border
back to the United States before I came out, but a doctor,
a fellow passenger, said it was no use keeping me in. So I
was born in Canadian territory. Or was I? This became
quite a tug-of-war, since it was not absolutely certain
where the train had been at the moment of my birth.
Naturally, Mom and Dad insisted that they had crossed
the border just in time.

Canada kept challenging this – and it made the papers, caused quite a ruckus. Dad – who was already famous at the time, and in the prime of his literary powers
– presented lengthy appeals to his literary friends here
and there, then moved on to his local political chums,
and finally appealed to the State Department, all to no

avail. I was a citizen of Canada. I was to remain a citizen of Canada until I came of age to start new paperwork all over again.

When I handed in my Canadian passport to the Canadian ambassador, he ripped it up in my face, and ever since Canada has never been happy with me.

Chapter 4

I am not sure which came first, but as Rashi says, there is no before or after.

I was in Hollywood doing some second unit work when Katrina Interlante walked over after something had happened and said "there's something going on between us," which was news to me, welcome news, but news. She flashed me that smile that we all know from her movies and she gave her tush that swivel and that did it for me. I was floored. I dream about her practically every night. We keep in touch...and promises have been made. We have to remember never to pass up a chance to have sex with a movie princess.

Katrina keeps reminding me that I saved her life, or performed something heroic for her, but I can't seem to remember what it was that was so terrific. Well, she is an actress, an artist, and they have different temperaments than we do, the rest of us. They see things in terms of drama and are moved to laughter or tears without much urging or without much really happening. I know the type and it can be tough to keep up.

I know something is going to get settled between us and I am not quite sure how I feel about her and how deep I want this to get. There is that movie that I may get to direct for her and if that comes about it could get difficult on the set. I am not sure about the movie, either.

So often these plans don't work out. Sometimes they do, of course.

Throughout the years, before I got married, I did have sex with actresses and actresses in New York are different from actresses in Hollywood. But in neither case is it for keeps. Promises are made but seldom kept. In New York they want relationships. In Hollywood they want love, love everlasting. I can't seem to remember how it ended with all of them, but apparently nobody got hurt, or hurt too badly.

I read all about them, my former lovers, on Page Six or on Facebook. Most of them are happily married and divorced. They complain about the paparazzi but are equally quick to tell everything about themselves. There is no shame. These days every life is an open book. There are no secrets. I keep being asked to "share," but I don't. I do not stay in touch as I should, and I feel guilty about this, too.

My wife Barbara and I are splits, separated. She blamed it on the horses. I blamed it on her mother. Her mother buried three husbands, and done with that, she got started on me. There is nothing worse than being judged through the eyes of a mother-in-law, and when a wife sticks to her mother it's like she never got married but only left home for a while....like taking a cruise.

Barbara says I keep being led into temptation, words of judgment straight from the wisdom of her mother.

There's worse.

I am compulsively inhibited, along with being a compulsive gambler (let's face the facts), but it's sure to get nasty now that most of the money is gone (to the horses) over a documentary project I promised to do for Adolf Gruberman. He gave. I took. This man is big, one of the world's leading industrialists and anti-Semites, and he's going to want his money back, or a completed film, but I have no intention of even starting that film. That's ridiculous.

I've been putting him off, going on about the dental work I need to get done, and that part is the truth, if partly. I've been having serious toothaches. The dentists keep sending me around one to another and some won't even talk to me anymore, first because I'm not taking the pills and second because I'm not paying the bills. I will need an oral surgeon.

"I will only wait so long," Gruberman keeps saying, or as I like to call him to his face, Adolf. He gave me the $250,000 for the project. Since there's not much left of that, I may have to ask him for more and that won't be pleasant. He could make trouble but I am used to trouble. I know the type. His e-mails to me are borderline threats. Once in a while he shows up in Greenwich Village where I've also been doing some second unit work.

He also owns newspapers and websites, Gruberman, does. He likes to say that I've absconded with all his money and that *there will be lawyers.*

I have not used up *all* his money. Don't believe everything you read.

Right now I'm in talks with Hollywood about doing that feature film and that could save the day.

Katrina Interlante is seeing to this and whatever Katrina wants Katrina gets.

She's in touch with the studio boss himself, Drake Goldsmith, on my behalf. I was on the phone to him not long ago.

The call came from him to me, which proved Katrina to be the studio's number one power.

So if I do gamble occasionally, or more than most, there is an upside.

I give money to charity, but keep word of it to myself because it's sinful to be proud of your good deeds.

The urge for this comes from my upbringing. I've given thousands to Save the Children Fund and thousands to Save the Horses Fund and you won't read that in the papers. I support Torah Study in Israel. I am not Jewish, but it serves him right, Adolf. I've used his money for all that and more. Adolf Gruberman is big on those divestments and those boycotts and those sanctions against Israel and he *is* Jewish.

Well, he was Jewish but has since converted.

Gruberman, I happen to know, pays for campus uprisings against Jewish students and he funds intifadas. I happen to know this.

He funds those university hate-fests against Israel at universities here and abroad.

I hear he's worth maybe $20 billion. He is, obviously, one of the richest men in the world. He can buy people and he can buy *wars*.

He can't buy peace.

Am I worried when he shows up at my Greenwich Village job? Not me, but the director, Carlos Loomis, is worried plenty.

"I don't like him around," he tells me.

"I can't stop him."

"Makes me nervous."

Especially when he shows up with those two goons.

Gruberman has been known to ruin people who get on his bad side. He does not kill them necessarily. He ruins their reputation, and that's worse.

Ruin a man's good name and there is nothing left.

My buddy Jay Garfield keeps reminding me that Adolf Gruberman does not ruin people with bullets. He kills them with *ink*.

He uses his newspaper like Julius Streicher used *Der Sturmer* back in Germany to inflame anti-Semitism and it seems to be working again.

Chapter 5

"They're trying to starve us to death," said my dad.

"Oh stop that nonsense," said my mom.

"Get us out of this place, Gil," said Dad.

This was a good place, or so I had thought when we all agreed to have them move out of that big house on Long Island. My sister Karen vouched for Kessinger's Communal Living Estates, run by Charles Kessinger, who proclaimed himself mayor of the spread, built for men and women 55-plus who were seeking "the good life in their golden years."

"I was in the administrative offices to complain about the lack of hot water," said Dad, "and I heard a secretary say they were running out of death certificates."

"Well," said Mom. "What do you expect? This is no kindergarten."

"Have you seen the dieting room?"

Actually I had and it was strange. People were sitting there along those tables with some bread, some fruits, some vegetables and some milk.

They seemed undernourished and dehydrated.

"Nobody is forced," said Mom.

"Our food is rationed. Can you deny that, Syl?"

My mom's name was Sylvia. Dad was Joseph Gilels, the famous writer, once upon a time. He was 82. Mom was 78.

Dad was Jewish. Mom was Presbyterian. I was caught in the middle, but they had always been in love, and still were.

Mom couldn't deny that; yes, the food was rationed.

"But only because of doctor's orders," she said. "They know what's best."

That's what the brochures said..."strict dietary observance for the continued well-being of your loved ones."

"They're experimenting with us," said Dad.

Only after we'd moved them in did I happen to check out the gym. Two scrawny old men, late 80s for sure, were in there, in the ring, fighting, and for real. Quite disturbing, a sight like this. Young guys, sure. I'm big on the sweet science. But old men on spindly legs should not be pounding each other to smithereens.

I asked the attendant why he wasn't stopping this and he said it's part of Kessinger's regimen for keeping fit. I had no choice but to believe him because we had already put down the $42,000. I paid most of it, and that was only a down payment. Karen was a psychiatrist, successful, but she and her husband had mortgages and all that and were awaiting their third child.

I had also visited the Bingo room and it was as depressing as all the rest. I thought it was only depressing. Dad thought it was dangerous.

I was starting to believe him, but when Karen and I, and back then, Barbara, checked out other nursing homes, they were just as bad or seemingly worse, and Kessinger's was no nursing home. No, it was a village with its own golf greens and swimming pools though I seldom saw anyone golfing or swimming. There were doctors and nurses round the clock. There were plenty of those, doctors and nurses, and ordinarily that would be understandable in a place like this, but so many of them? Residents who were here one day were gone the next. Moving vans in great numbers were in and out of the bungalows each time we came to visit.

This other part was tricky. One of the residents told me, "Everybody needs a pass to leave and nobody gets a pass."

"Mayor" Charles Kessinger confirmed this when I asked him, and he was right when he said that's how it works everywhere under "controlled environments."

All nursing homes operated by such strict rules; can't have the elderly, say with Alzheimer's, just taking off, can we?

Kessinger's – Kessinger told me – had to operate by the same rules. Would I want my mom and dad up and gone one day?

Made sense.

Dad was approaching Alzheimer's, though, I'd say, more than half the time he was lucid. He was still the same tough fighter and tough writer. He'd written seven bestsellers and was often the *New Yorker's* talk of the town. He was known around the world and was said to be on the short list for a Nobel. He was a grand old man, my dad, and Mom had stuck with him, unconditionally, from day one.

Quite a couple, my mom and dad.

Now this!

Kessinger explained that he'd stopped the casino tours because some of them refused to go back.

That was another reason for the controls.

They imprison you for growing old?

I asked him that and he said I had much to learn. These were the facts, the facts of life.

My mom and dad were living a fact of life.

Karen, my sister, did not visit often enough and this caused some friction between us. I visited once a week when I was in town. When I was out of town and she'd be filling in, she'd say, cheerfully, that they were doing fine. No problem. That's because Dad put up a good front and never told her what he told me.

"They restrict the hours when we can watch television," Dad said.

"Two hours isn't enough?" said Mom.

"Why restrict anything?" said Dad.

"They know what they're doing," said Mom.

"Precisely my point," said Dad. "They know precisely what they're doing."

There was also a computer room in the recreation center, and this too was restricted, for one hour a day.

Police were on constant patrol. They were friendly, but they were police.

Every time I came here I felt guilty. I felt guilty before I came here, while I was here, and after I left. Two people who'd been so strong, so vibrant, and so self-sufficient all their lives were now at the mercy of powers beyond them, and all that because at a certain hour they had grown old. To get them out of here would cost another fortune, but I would have to get them out. Dad's complaints about this place were starting to ring true...and Dad had never been a complainer.

Dad knew the documentary I was making for Adolf Gruberman, or rather the film I wasn't making for Adolf Gruberman.

"Take every cent from that mamzer," he said.

Dad knew the business. He'd had his own skirmishes with Hollywood. Three of his books had been made into films. All three were "boffo" box office but he was never happy with the results. He kept his opinions mostly to himself. "You can't impose one form of art upon another," he told me, so if he was disappointed he wasn't disillusioned. "Besides, the check cleared."

He still had dreams and he still typed away on an old Underwood and once a month Shirley, who'd been his Girl Friday since forever, came over to pick up the pages. He'd won a Pulitzer but still thought his Big Book was ahead of him. Mom encouraged this. I asked her if she was doing it just to keep him from falling apart, and she said, no, he still had his gifts.

He was a great man, my dad. He once told me the secret to his success. "Sylvia," he said. My mom. "I got lucky, but don't tell her I said that," he'd chuckle.

I finally read his books much later on. He had warned me not to touch them until I was old enough. When I was old enough I was surprised that Dad really matched the greats of the past. A regular Hemingway? My dad? But I wasn't prepared for the sex. Dad spared no details and some of it was too intimate and too raw for the eyes of a son.

Actually, Dad had written eight novels. Yes, eight. But he was reluctant to go ahead with the Ninth. He was afraid it would bring about his death. Beethoven had died after his Ninth Symphony. The superstition, upon a Ninth work of art, ran deep among composers; Mahler and Bruckner were terrified after they'd completed their eight symphonies. I kept assuring Dad that nine was a lucky number, and it sure did no harm to Gordie Howe, and it certainly did no harm to Maurice "Rocket" Richard.

But Dad was still worried...but still had no choice except to persist with his Ninth novel. He was a writer, after all.

Dad didn't know he was famous worldwide until he was 60. That's when he travelled to England to meet with his foreign agents. They had invited him over for business. Thousands were waiting for him at the airport. He knew that his books were recognized but fame for himself had never been on his mind and in fact he scorned fame. He claimed to be unhappy about that rock star reception, but Mom told me that he was really pleased. "Everybody wants to be adored," she said. "Your dad, God love him, is no saint."

We knew he mustn't be disturbed when he stepped into his sanctuary to do his writing. He'd shower, get himself dressed up in his finest suit and tie, and get started. He wasn't extraordinarily vain, so, when I was young, I asked him why he had to go so formal just to write. He had no plans to leave the house, not when he wrote. "Writing is holy," he said.

Every writer, he said, writes his own bible.

After years of plenty came five years of famine and Dad lost everything. Certainly not everything, but it was pretty bad.

Chapter 6

Barbara – living apart but still legally my wife – showed up at my apartment on 72nd Street as if there was nothing on her mind.

"How is everything?" she said, looking around disapprovingly.

"I don't know," I said.

"Hah!" she laughed. "Do you care?"

She used to accuse me of not caring about anything – besides the gambling. I cared plenty. I even cared for her. I still loved her.

I thought she still loved me.

I was in no mood to go round again on all that and she seemed to want to talk something *out* maybe. The talking had already been done, for about two years, and after that she left me. Or maybe I left her. It was never quite clear what had happened. Well It was quite clear, after all. She had an affair. She liked to say that I drove her out because of the gambling but I knew that to be partly true; mostly true was a fellow critic she had met at the Manhattan Academy of Drama, James Headley.

She taught a course specifically on the writing of criticism and she was a critic herself, quite famous. I never understood why people had to learn to be critics. I thought we were all critics automatically. I thought criticism came with the territory, human nature. She had a syndicated radio show where the talk was mostly books and movies, or anything under the sun.

"I wish you wouldn't keep mentioning my name," I said.

She kept bringing me up. She did not mention my name when her guest, an expert on compulsion, got to talking about compulsive gambling. He had the statistics and I knew the statistics. We are all vulnerable and the figures show that 40 million of us are compulsive gamblers at one level or another. That's all? Doesn't everybody buy lottery tickets?

Those of us who play the horses, mostly, are the least of the problem.

"I can sue," I said, "if you keep it up."

Usually she'd come back with some smarty remark, but she had something else cooking.

She wondered if I'd agree to be a guest on her show.

"I'm serious," she said.

"To talk about what?"

"Forgiveness," she said.

"I don't know anything about the subject."

"You've never faced that situation?"

"I don't know. I can't remember."

"It's one of the blessings of being human," she said.

She said forgiveness was a gift denied all other creatures.

"What brings this up?" I asked.

"It's a topic never mentioned, not publicly."

For Jews, their God had 13 Attributes of Compassion. For Christians, one, Jesus, was enough.

We all want forgiveness. Some want it even *before* they've committed the transgression.

Can people really forgive or is this strictly God's business?

It's the same on punishment. Sometimes (or so we're taught) God doesn't punish until that person or that nation's "cup of iniquity" has been filled.

Did Beethoven, then, all alone save latter-day Germany with his merits and his divine musical attributes?

I had been at my desk checking the latest racing results when she showed up. My heart always beat faster at the sight of her. Her smiles melted me. I mustn't show this, though. We were supposed to be at odds. What a shame. What a waste. She made me coffee without my asking. I kept busy to my task, but thought I heard her sniffling in the kitchen. I assumed things weren't going so well between herself and her lover, James Headley. His was a big name among academics, and that was another thing, I wasn't intellectual enough for her. I knew what I was talking about, she liked to say, except I didn't care much for her friends. That was no lie.

I could talk books, movies, culture, politics, but I preferred the company of horseplayers and boxing fans. I bet on boxing, too.

I lost a ton on the fights. I also bet baseball and football; never basketball. I couldn't even name the teams in basketball.

There were too many teams altogether in all sports, enough to drive you crazy. You couldn't cover them all, as much as you tried.

I was not compulsive, never mind what they said. They said it all day even as they rushed to the convenience store to fill up on lottery tickets.

I played the lotteries, too, but that was not my game and a game that relied purely on luck was not my game.

I was a professional. I was scientific about my gambling. Let them talk. I was once talked into attending a

GA meeting, Gamblers Anonymous, and the stories really were horrific, but none of that applied to me. I was never that far gone. Most of them were separated or divorced because of the gambling and, I learned, as if I didn't know, that where once upon a time gambling used to be a man's world or a man's "vice," women had gained equality here too thanks to the lotteries and the slot machines.

The goal I had set for myself was sure to please nobody…and it probably entered my mind, something like a flash, like an epiphany, on that day when I had won every race on the card. *I could not lose.* Every bob of the head at the wire finished in my favor. I sat myself down for a long talk and after some debate decided to phase out my filmmaking as much as possible and turn to horse playing professionally, or semi-professionally.

I would turn off all the other noise and make myself singular and ruthless and even compulsive in pursuit of excellence at one task and one task alone. I would be as compulsive as Beethoven had been to music, as Fischer had been to chess, as Ted Williams had been to hitting, as Salinger had been to writing, as David Lean had been to filming. That was the plan.

For some reason, on this day, Barbara wasn't giving me the high hand. There was a new seriousness about her, almost to the edge of sincerity. Where were the snappy comebacks, the quick one-liners, the sophisticated wisecracks? She'd been born rich and she had rich tastes and we met before I got into film, when I was a newspaper reporter, and she'd been pursued by the smartest and the sharpest, but she chose me instead and she never stopped reminding me how lucky I was.

For a time this was true. Even Mom and Dad were nuts about her. She was good-hearted, they said, and this was also true. She cared about global warming, about female genital mutilation in Africa and even here in the United States among the newly arrived, and she cared about the entire human race. That's a big world out there to be worried about and that is bound to crowd out a husband.

She visited my folks more often than I did over at the 55-plus community and brought them gifts. I wasn't supposed to know.

She gave her time voluntarily to immigrants learning English and citizenship.

"I hear you've been having problems," she said joining me at my desk and showing leg.

"The usual," I said.

"I mean your teeth," she said. "I can tell you're in pain."

"The doctors say that the swelling has to go down first before they can do any pulling."

"But you refuse to take the pills, right?"

"Right."

"This could get serious, you know."

"That's what they say."

"But you don't care. I think you have a death wish, Gil. I always knew that about you. That's why you gamble, even though you know you can't win."

"I DO WIN."

"Still chasing those four numbers?"

"Is this why you're here, Barbara?"

Still no fancy backtalk when, after a pause, she said, "I still think about you."

"I know you still talk about me."

"Well you are famous."

"For what!"

She laughed.

"You once said there's no beginning and no end."

"I did?"

"Yes you did."

"I said there's no before and after. I got that from Rashi. What's your point?"

"Just that life doesn't always follow a neat pattern," she said.

"Shit happens?"

"Well it does."

"Mistakes were made, right?"

"Mistakes were made, Gil. Yes. Mistakes were made."

She stepped for the door, stopped, and gave me a look I'd never seen before, a look that said something between pity and adoration.

"Think about that," she said softly.

"About what?"

"What we talked about."

"My death wish? My gambling?"

"About forgiveness."

Chapter 7

Over at the racing room I took the seat that I had regularly reserved. There's nothing like this. Only horseplayers know what it's like early afternoon before the races have begun and ahead anything can happen and there you are, ready for the action and for the thrill of beating the odds. Every race was sure to be an adventure. I had done my handicapping overnight. I had my horses picked out after deciding to focus on one track, Gulfstream.

There wasn't much of a crowd today and I liked it better like this, although there was always one degenerate yelling his lungs out as if that would make a difference. I had no friends here, no pals, no racetrack chums, except for true friends that I knew from off-track. That was, for me at least, always a distraction, and once you made a racetrack buddy he expected you to share tips with him and share bets with him and that never ended well. I did have acquaintances.

I liked Gulfstream because the better horses were there and thus the better riders. This day's bankroll was $400 and I decided to do nothing fancy. I just wanted to make a few thousand and so I would be smart for a change. I would bet only the two stakes races that came up later on, the eighth and the ninth, and put all my money on just four horses, two in each race, and only to

win and place. No doubles today, no exactas, and no tri-
fectas. None of these exotics. Not today – and no numbers. I'd go strictly by my handicapping. I had spent four
hours doing the handicapping so I had my horses picked
out scientifically.

I would bet none of the early races, the cheap races,
but wait, sit back and wait, and then strike. That would
mean waiting nearly five hours. I ordered a drink and
started feeling all right. The races started and as expected the favorites kept coming in and that could be a
bad sign for the rest of the card, or it could be a good
sign, meaning that it was time for the longshots to start
coming in. I only bet longshots.

Smiley the Mooch came over and asked if I had anything good.

"No, Smiley, not today."

"Can you spare a ten?"

I gave him a 20.

Smiley's house had been destroyed by Hurricane
Sandy. The boys all around tried to give him a hand. No
one could recall him ever winning a single race.

I watched a few races. Smiley kept yelling, "I told you
that horse would win. I told you!" He always said that
after he'd named every horse as the winner.

I grew restless for all that waiting and stepped out to
go to the bathroom, but right there was the craps table,
hot with action, and so I stepped up and put down $100
and it was gone in a flash. I went back to the racing room
knowing that I had to make back that $100. I was abso-
lutely not going to do anything before the eighth race,
but now I had no choice. So I bet the favorite in the sixth
race, a sure thing everybody said, and when Smiley the
Mooch started rooting for him leaving the gate, I knew I

was a goner and tore up my ticket. The horse finished second to last.

Now I was down to $200, so I had to make up another two hundred to get me back to $400 to get those bets down on the horses I'd labored on all last night. So I put down my last $200 on another favorite in the seventh race, and I asked Smiley, I begged Smiley, to please not tell me whom he bet. Made no difference. This time the horse did not finish second to last, but last. Barbara would call this the Anatomy of a Horseplayer.

Next morning I tried not reading the paper to find out if those horses I'd picked out, and never bet, had won – and yes they had.

Chapter 8

Carlos Loomis ran his production studio in Margate, New Jersey, which made it convenient for me, or quite unfortunate, depending on the day. I was his editor, his cutter. He liked to do most of it himself, but when I was around he'd use me, and he paid well. We had our problems. Some staffers thought we had a personality clash. He was doing that film, that documentary, about life in the 1960s centered around Greenwich Village, so that's where he was most days, with his crew, which should have included me. This was not a job where you punched a clock.

I showed up at his studio, which was only 10 minutes from where I had just been, and there were only a few people around.

"Carlos kept asking for you."

"He could have called."

"Not my problem."

I called and he said that there were six films that still needed editing, but he'd prefer that I go back to New York to do some second unit work.

I said, "Okay."

"I'm glad it's okay," he said.

When I got there Adolf Gruberman was there, and there was no work getting done.

"He is shutting us down," said Carlos.

He can do this? Yes he can. He can do this because he filed a complaint with the City about an unauthorized license. Loomis was in no position to counter. He employed undocumented workers and though New York was relaxed about this, Carlos couldn't take the chance. He couldn't put those people at risk. Gruberman was waiting for me on the curb at his limo. He was there without his thugs, for some reason.

"Now what?" Carlos asked me.

"I'll take care of this," I said.

"When? Every day costs money."

"I know how to handle this."

"You owe him money?"

"Something like that," I said.

"The gambling?"

"Not exactly."

"That's so cliché," Carlos said.

"It's something else."

"Whatever it is, get it fixed."

I couldn't tell him what it really was between Gruberman and me. I couldn't tell anyone except for a few people that Gruberman was paying me to do an anti-Israel film and that I had taken the money under false pretenses to pay off gambling losses. I would never make a film like that, but I kept stringing him along, the anti-Semitic bastard. He kept reminding me to "lay it on thick."

I had already hired a few actors to fake it up if the time came to show him a few minutes of film. I got them throwing stones at Israeli soldiers. I had an old woman cry, weeping terribly, that the Israelis had stolen her home. That took several takes because she kept laughing and she couldn't speak Arabic, this actress. She was Spanish. I said that was close enough. I had them marching with signs saying Death to Israel. I had put up a notice at Brooklyn College asking for volunteers to shout slogans that compared Jews to Nazis for what they were doing to the poor Palestinians – and so many volunteers showed up that I had to turn a few hundred of them away. They laid it on thick all on their own. They left behind leaflets urging everybody to divest from Israel.

Adolf Gruberman would like this.

I was told that I could go to any college campus and get thousands to volunteer for an Israel-bashing movie, and not just students, but professors as well.

I was in the right business if I wanted to go ahead with this.

I even got phone calls from professors asking when I was going to do my next round of filming. They had anti-Israel speeches they could make.

Those could be taken directly from their lectures. Whenever I'd be ready, they told me, they'd be ready.

Some read their speeches and their lectures over the phone and urged me to read their editorials in *The New York Times*.

Word was spreading. I was getting swamped. I was starting to get phone calls from Iran and Saudi Arabia. They all wanted in on the act.

I was directed to a particular imam in the United States who could give a fiery anti-Israeli rant that was singular for its venom. He was adept at calling Israelis dogs and, for the same price, he could add that Americans were pigs. I heard from people who said they were connected to Hamas, the Palestinian Authority and Islamic Jihad. They also wanted in. Nobody wanted to be left out.

I heard from people who told me there were such things as professional protesters. They could arrive any place as flash mobs. If I checked around, I was informed, I would find that hating Israel and hating all Jews into the bargain was a national and international profession, an industry, a business, big business. At a university in Ramallah, I was told, special accredited courses were offered to teach students how to riot against Israel, and reporters were given instructions on how to report against Israel.

Ramallah – that was the Palestinian territory where two IDF kids wandered in accidentally and got lynched from a police station.

I was advised to cover Israel Apartheid Week, an event used to denounce Israel along a thousand campuses; something like Spring Break for anti-Semites.

From all over the world I received congratulations and best wishes now that word had leaked out (through Adolf Gruberman's grapevine) that I was preparing a film against Israel. What can we do? How can we help? Our services are at your disposal. Donations – real money – started to come in, most of it from anonymous sources. I received bank transfers as small as $25 and as big as $10,000.

I used every cent of that money for Jewish charities and to pay off my gambling debts.

There'd been threats on my life if I didn't go through with the film, or, if I showed any sympathy for the Jews.

There was one side to the story and one side only.

Through emails I was approached by people who asked if they needed a screen test in order to shout "kill the Jews" for the camera. I was informed that there were actors here and throughout the world who had already acted in many anti-Israel films and were always ready to do so again, if I would please give them a hearing. They had material ready to go.

They all knew Adolf Gruberman, of course.

His anti-Semitism ran deep. It was impossible to know what turned people like that; Stockholm Syndrome? He was not the only one to have changed colors and it did appear to be an epidemic. They were small in number, but loud, and entirely hateful. Gruberman had others doing those kinds of films, pure propaganda, and he had a particular reason for including me.

He wanted me to marry his daughter. He knew I was separated from Barbara, but even before that he had his eye on me as the perfect match for Helen, the daughter who couldn't find a mate. She was not attractive. Well, there were plenty like that and there was always someone for someone but for some reason it refused to click for Helen, and Helen was the love of his life.

So I had that much over him, so he could push, but he wouldn't dare push me too far. Apparently I was Helen's last resort.

Gruberman took me to his club for dinner. I couldn't eat much because of my tooth. I ordered steak but could only take a few bites.

Instead I drank, vodka and tonic, and even that hurt. I had started drinking, maybe because I couldn't eat.

"I don't mean to get so heavy-handed," he said, nearly apologetic.

He wanted a progress report and I told him that I was still casting.

"I gave you people," he said.

He gave me professional rabble-rousers.

"I need actors."

"I know people all over the world."

"I don't want stone throwers."

"I even gave you Israeli actors."

Yes, he did, and they were bad actors and bad Israelis. They hated their own people.

"Amateurs," I said, forgetting to mention everything else.

"Why do you need professionals?"

"Because I'm a professional," I said.

"Have you even scouted locations?"

"Glad you brought that up. I may need more money."

"More money?"

"More money," I said.

"Show me something first."

"More money first."

"I'll think about it," he said.

Then he said, "You should come around once in a while."

"Sure."

"Helen has lost a lot of weight."

"Oh, I hadn't noticed, I mean I hadn't noticed that she needed to, I mean lose weight."

"She lost a lot of weight, you know."

"Give her my best."

"It wouldn't hurt you to come around," he said. "You know she's always had a crush on you. She's a fine girl."

"Everybody knows that," I said.

"Our door is always open."

"I'll need you to set this straight, about Carlos Loomis."

"I'll think about it," he said.

"He had nothing to do with this," I said.

"Have you been gambling again?"

"What's the difference?"

"I have an investment in you," he said.

"My personal life is personal."

"So what's with Barbara?"

"I just said, that's my business."

"You're not divorced yet, I hear."

"I hear this, too."

"I hear you lost at the casino yesterday."

"Says who?"

"I got spies."

Yes he did.

"I need you to fix this with Carlos Loomis."

"I need you to make me a MOVIE."

Chapter 9

Carlos Loomis was back in Margate. He couldn't film in Greenwich Village now and get it authentic, so now he had to settle for second best on a sound stage. This didn't make him happy. He was blaming me, for some reason. "I knew it would come to this," he said. I felt pretty rotten. I had brought this on. I had brought this on, Adolf Gruberman, on both our heads.

"Give me time to straighten this out," I promised.

Where was it I read that a crooked thing can't be made straight? King Solomon, I think.

Carlos still did not know what business I had with Gruberman. I was hesitant to tell him. I did not know what side he was on and these days everybody was on one side or the other, politically. There was no middle ground. People had stopped talking and started shouting. Along the Internet, now everybody had his 15 minutes of fame, and then some.

"You put me in a bad spot," he said.

I felt terrible.

But he couldn't fire me because he needed a man who could cut film, an editor, and the other guy usually showed up drunk.

"Let's see what happens," I said.

"It already did."

Some people just don't get along.

Chapter 10

Katrina Interlante weaved her magic and got me an interview with Drake Goldsmith. She kept her promise. Of all my brief encounters from the past, there was still none like Katrina, for Hollywood. I'd drop anything for her and all it took was a few words, a few looks, and I was hooked. For some reason, though, I kept thinking about Barbara.

The call came from my agent, Mandy Marcus.

"The head of the studio wants a meeting."

"I can't make it," I told him, first because I already had a job, editing for Carlos Loomis, whom I cannot keep disappointing – though he was a prick besides.

"Fuck him and come on over. This is no joke. I made the reservations for you at the Four Seasons and the meeting's been set."

Next I told him that I had dentist appointments to keep for an infection that had gotten pretty bad. I was in constant pain and wouldn't be much use talking deals.

"Shmuck," he said. "You'll be here."

I should not be meeting anyone with this affliction of mine, but when Hollywood calls, you go. This was to be my first feature film, my big chance. Every director in town wanted a shot to remake that film that got it all wrong from the novel. It was time to do the book justice. I had met the author of the book, then done a treatment and a screenplay, all of which gave me an edge. Out there documentarians had to prove themselves worthy for full-length dramas. We were thought to be not quite ready for big time. We were practically starting from scratch.

This re-make had been in the works for five years. The studio kept putting it off, mostly because the top brass kept being reshuffled. The new head was Drake Goldsmith. Over the past few months there'd been hints that the project was being brought back to life. Even Page Six said so. Mandy kept telling me that Drake Goldsmith liked my documentaries, liked my treatment, liked my screenplay, so to stay tuned.

Good news?

That was too much to hope for. I knew the competition and I knew Hollywood. There was always talk. Most times nothing happened.

But we keep dreaming.

So finally, just when you least expected it and just when things were at their worst, here was that call, obviously at Katrina's backstage maneuvers.

So I was there, all right.

Drake Goldsmith started off by saying that he'd be happier if we could eliminate the politics and the religion.

"Does the other guy really have to be an Arab?"

"That's in the book," I said.

"But we're making a movie."

"In that case we're making the Redford movie again. So why bother?"

Mandy gave me a look. He knew I was salivating for this job, so why the attitude? We were meeting at the coffee shop at the Four Seasons in Beverly Hills and not a word was said about my disfigured condition. On the plane I had bitten into some peanuts that landed square on that bad tooth. Along with that came unbearable pain and a surge of swelling.

Now the smell of food made me gag.

Drake Goldsmith was about my age, in his early 40s. He was wearing a suit and tie, not quite Hollywood, but it gave him gravitas. He had fast-moving blue eyes, was going bald, and he had a somewhat oval face, which made it appear that he still had some baby-fat to shed and was only beginning to work himself into a tycoon. He had not been taken seriously at the start. He had come up from commercial television, had even made commercials, but that's what sold these days. He had three hits in a row, now as head of the studio. So nobody was denying him anymore.

"Let's put that aside for the moment," Drake said.

"Yes," my agent Mandy Marcus agreed. "Let's drop that for the moment."

Mandy Marcus was having pancakes and Drake Goldsmith was having eggs over easy and each time they took a mouthful another waiter would come over on tip-toes with fresh linen. Drake was so busy with the eating and the slurping and the gulping and the burping, that I thought it would fall to me to remind him why we're here in the first place.

I was still waiting for the good news. I'd been waiting for it the moment Mandy announced it over the phone, without the details, and I'd been waiting for it on the plane, nauseous, bleeding gums, dizzy spells and all, remembering to forget my troubles but to stay focused on good news. This was supposed to be a tonic, good news.

"We'd like your thoughts on the casting of Josh."

I said that I was glad we were using the character's real name, as it appears in the novel. That was the whole point of the re-make, to be true to the novel. I had spent some time with the novelist. He was a recluse, but he knew my dad. I was surprised that he was not disappointed or even disillusioned on what finally came up on the screen from his words on paper. "They're children," he told me. "Who complains about children?"

He had no fantasies about Hollywood getting it right.

He was indifferent about having a second try at his novel. "Sure. Why not?" He cared only about writing. Movies weren't his business.

"It's all luck anyway," he said.

He really didn't give a damn about anything except for the purity of writing. No wonder he was friends with Dad.

For years there'd been talk, even in places as far as Russia, about getting a movie done based exactly on the novel – the political correctness be damned.

His novel – with a million dollar temptation at the center – was a big hit, and controversial. The novel was great and the novelist had hit a nerve.

There was a poor Jew with a beautiful wife and a rich Arab who wanted the wife, if only for one night. That is where the million dollars comes in.

The Jewish character wasn't really poor. But he was working too hard just to stay middle class. His name was Joshua Kane.

The Arab was an oil rich billionaire. His name was Ibrahim Hassan and he was not portrayed stereotypically.

The novelist had made them pretty equal as adversaries.

But the book was still controversial. This was more than just two men struggling over a woman. This was two histories doing battle.

That's why the first version, the Redford version, skipped all that; to avoid the politics and to keep eyes on the money, the sex and the box office.

Joan was the desired one, highborn, blonde and extraordinarily classy and beautiful.

"So what do you think?" Drake Goldsmith asked me at the Four Seasons coffee shop, about the casting of Josh.

I wasn't sure I had heard right.

"What do you think?" he repeated.

Mandy gave me another look.

"What do you think, Gil?"

I was stupefied by what I had just heard.

"We think of it as reverse casting," Drake said.

That it was, sure was. More than that – it was *in your face* casting.

"You brought me here for a joke?" I said.

Mandy was worried. He put down his fork and stopped eating. Drake took me in stride. He was a cool customer.

"I knew you'd need time to think this over," he said.

Mandy let it be known that I was not the only director being considered. I needed to think this over carefully.

"Let's not put pressure on the man," Drake said.

I asked Drake if this was do or die for me.

"Depends on how seriously you want to make this film, and how serious you are about switching over to feature films."

I never liked it when short films or documentary films were deemed incidental. We were journalists. We went to places where even fiction wouldn't go.

"There isn't much time to waste," said Mandy.

Other studios and other producers were likewise in a mood to buy the rights.

"We don't want this going cold," Drake agreed.

True. Hollywood ran hot and cold and you had to catch it when it was hot. Once it cooled off it rarely came round again. You could be doomed if you let the moment pass. You wanted this, I kept thinking. Yes you did. But do you want it that badly? Well, yes...but. This would be some compromise. No, it would be a complete sell-out. But to whom do I owe my loyalty? Plenty. You owe plenty. Never mind your own integrity. Integrity? Did someone say integrity?

But imagine, a feature film all my own. Studio backing. A hundred million dollar budget, most likely. Oscars. Red Carpet.

The envelope, please, for the biggest cave-in of all time.

I asked if I was in automatically if I agreed.

"I can't promise that one hundred percent," Drake said.

"Nothing is one hundred percent," Mandy said.

"But you would have a big edge," Drake said.

"That's for sure," Mandy said.

"I've already been approached by several whale directors," Drake said.

Spielberg? Scorsese? Tarantino?

"Even with this casting?" I said.

"Especially with this casting," said Mandy.

Drake asked me what I was working on right now – as if he didn't know. Mandy had surely filled him in.

I told him.

"I see," he said slowly.

So this was the good news. No, this was the great news. Mandy should have known better and he should have told me over the phone, but then, of course, I would not have made the trip. I would have stayed in New York with my toothache. Instead I was here with my toothache pondering an offer that was hard to accept or refuse.

Mandy knew I was desperate, but was I *that* desperate? He also knew that I gambled and that I was always in a fix.

I knew how persuasive they could be, studio heads and producers, when they caught you in between jobs.

On the other hand, is there a director willing to walk into a job guaranteed to make him a laughingstock?

This was so risky that it could easily backfire...never mind the tastelessness of it all.

So here we go again. I was up to my neck in this back in New York. I didn't have to come to Hollywood.

"Josh was a soldier in the Israeli army," I reminded them both. "He was a passionate Zionist. This would be a mockery."

"Strong words," said Mandy.

"This would be a travesty," I added to pile on another strong word.

"Think of the buzz," said Mandy.

"That's exactly what I *was* thinking."

"We ran this by nearly everyone at the studio," said Drake, "and most everybody thought of it as an inspiration."

I could imagine all the 23-year-old executives jumping all over this.

Sure. Why not? Mel Gibson playing a Jewish character. Brilliant! Cigars, everyone!

(Who really was behind all this – Adolf?)

Mandy, seeing how this was getting out of hand, suggested we give it a rest until next day. Drake agreed and we separated and I went up to my room. There was a knock at the door. Security. The lady in uniform politely asked if everything was okay. I said sure, why? The maids found blood all over the pillowcase. I assured Security that there had been no violence, just me and my bad tooth.

"Well okay," she said but not happy to find this happening in Beverly Hills. There were codes to live by in Beverly Hills.

They could always spot a New Yorker.

There'd been blood in the sink when I first got in the room. I hadn't given it a second thought, but now I rushed to phone Mandy.

"Was I bleeding at breakfast?"

"Profusely."

He misunderstood. I explained.

"Don't worry. Nothing like that except for your sanity."

"You should have warned me."

"You wouldn't have come."

"Well, you were just doing your job."

"What glories have you in New York right now?"

"I hear you."

"Let me tell you about life from my years as an agent."

"I have to hear this?"

"Life gives you one chance at a time."

"Wisdom of our Fathers."

"Tomorrow with bells on, buddy."

Next day it was dinner. So I was being wined and dined. What a waste. I took a bite of that bread and had to run to the bathroom to spit it out.

"You've had a night to sleep on this," said Drake Goldsmith.

No, I had a night to stay awake on this.

"So," I said. "We're being sensitive to the Arabs but not to the Jews."

"Politics can be deep shit," Drake said.

There'd been a thousand articles about Hollywood's cowardice on political minefields, such as Islam versus the West, so it was useless to go over it again.

Elsewhere filmmakers and even cartoonists were being targeted and even assassinated for touching that third rail of politics. I should know.

"I'll have to think about this," I said.

Mandy turned yellow.

Drake Goldsmith got to the point, polite no more:

"You New York guys make me sick. You think you're better than Hollywood but when the chips are down you come running to us for fast money."

Mandy came to my defense. "But Gil is turning down the fast money."

"Still with his nose in the air," said Drake.

"Let's calm down," said Mandy.

"I know I'm being a prick," said Drake. "But I'm tired of all that NYU crap. You guys make film. We make MOVIES."

Up came Katrina Interlante. She made the grand entrance you'd expect of a movie star. She was today's Lauren Bacall.

For some reason I was thinking about Barbara.

Katrina air kissed Mandy, hugged and kissed Drake but favored me with the works, hugs and kisses on the lips.

"You know I want that part," she said flirtatiously to Drake.

Was this a set-up?

"When do we start?" she asked me.

"We're talking," I said.

"I love Joan," she said.

Joan was the dish the two men were fighting over. In the first movie she was played by Demi Moore, who did fine as Demi Moore but not as Joan.

"She's such a strong character," Katrina said – and she was blonde, like Joan in the book. She could be perfect for the part.

"I saw the movie, but after reading the book," she said, "come on, it needs to be done right."

"We all agree on that," said Drake.

"You met the novelist?" she asked me.

"I spent a couple of days with him."

"I hear he's eccentric but a great writer."

"They're all nuts," I said.

"I knew some in New York. Everybody's a novelist in New York and everybody's a screenwriter in Hollywood."

Joan, she said, was the central character in the book, and was perhaps the most powerful female presence in any novel from anyone. She named Madame Bovary and Anna Karenina as competitive but no match. Joan was the woman of the 21st century. She knew how to use her sexuality – and had both those men fighting for her to the death, in the novel, not the movie, and that needed to be changed.

"I'm always fascinated to know what the novelist had in mind," she asked me.

"I asked him," I said, "and he said that the author is the last to know."

"Really."

"It's for everybody else to figure out and their opinions are more worthy than his."

"In a crazy way that makes sense."

"He did volunteer that if he had to give it one word, he'd come up with it, but only when facing a firing squad."

"What was that word?"

The author had told me that novelists hated to reduce their novels into synopses. What to leave out? If I could write the paragraph, he said, I would write the paragraph instead of the novel. His next novel, he said, would probably have to be tweeted, told in 140 characters or less.

"Come on," said Katrina. "What was the word?"

"Temptation. He said sex is nothing. Temptation is everything."

"Sex is nothing?"

"It's all about temptation."

"Forbidden fruit, huh?"

"Right."

"Fascinating."

She had to run and said ta-ta. Like those who went Hollywood from New York, she had smarts.

"That's a start," said Mandy.

"Fortuitous," said Drake.

"She's beautiful," I said.

"Well, I've had my say," said Drake.

"Your turn," said Mandy.

"I'll have to think it over," I said.

I already had thought it over and the answer was no, but you never wanted to go closing doors.

"As you wish," said Drake.

Katrina had slipped me a note.

Chapter 11

She had a place in Santa Monica.

"So sex is nothing?" she said seductively.

We were sitting on the sofa in one of her living rooms. A maid was cleaning up all around us, so busy and so close that I expected her to start dusting my hair. I wondered if Katrina kept her here in such proximity to avoid anything happening between us, and if so, what was the purpose of this invitation? Katrina wore something loose for slacks and something tight to reveal her nipples. A world full of men desired her, but I was here instead, or I was here in their place. The urge to subdue her – this could not be helped. She was a mystery that needed to be solved in bed.

I was crazy about her. She had accused me of being "wickedly handsome" as for her attraction to me and I liked the handsome but not the wicked part.

I offered the temptation defense, but you can talk about sex only for so long until something happens or nothing happens. I knew she wanted to get bookish and intellectual on the topic because I was a New Yorker and New Yorkers were supposed to be intellectual, typified by Marilyn Monroe's going for Arthur Miller. The maid kept cleaning and dusting and soon emerged with a vacuum cleaner, so that we had to shout.

Katrina wanted to know more about me and maybe I told her some but her nipples kept getting in the way. About herself, though I didn't ask, she came here from Russia when she was 10, specifically to make it in Hollywood when she came of age. She was brought over by her mother. Her father, a billionaire industrialist, remained back in Russia to fight off the government that was trying to divest him of his holdings and his wealth. He'd already spent three years in jail simply for being too rich and too powerful, which the Kremlin deemed a threat to its own might.

"Stage mom?" I said.

"Oh absolutely," she laughed.

Perfect – another mom to cast a dark shadow.

She still had the trace of a Russian accent, but she could switch accents for any role. The critics liked her and the public loved her.

But she felt insecure and undeserving of all that adulation. Every new part presented a new risk, a new chance to fail. In fact her latest movie had not done all that well either at the box office or among the reviewers. There was one particular critic in New York that detested her, Miles Korwin, and she wondered if I could put a stop to him, since I knew him. Yes I did know him. He was a gambler just like me, only with him it was the harness racing and I only knew the thoroughbreds, when they were running well.

"He's killing me," Katrina said about Miles, the son of a bitch.

"He kills everybody," I said.

"He never says anything good about me."

"That's why he's a critic."

"But you know it's personal and he's trying to ruin me."

Barbara knew him better than I did. She even has him on her radio show occasionally where they can ruin people together. Oh Barbara!

What to do about Barbara?

So Katrina was wondering if I could talk to Miles and ask him to back off and for a moment I wondered if that's what this was all about.

"Only if it's not too much trouble," she said, pouting.

"I'll see what I can do."

"Someone like that can finish your whole career," she said.

"I'll talk to him," I said, knowing that sometimes the approach can make it worse.

She gave me a kiss on the cheek, which was sore from the bad tooth.

She moved us into another parlor and this time another maid was cleaning up around us and we had to keep shouting.

"I started off modeling for Pierre Jacques," she said. "You've heard of him?"

"No. I don't travel in those circles."

"You are a moody person, aren't you?" she said.

"We all have moods."

"I think I'm in love with you," she shouted over the vacuum cleaner din.

I never knew how to answer this, from anyone. So I pretended not to hear.

"I was in love with him," she said, speaking of Pierre Jacques, so maybe that's what I heard in the first place.

I knew she'd been married twice and there were rumors about her and someone else.

"But I didn't marry him," she said.

"Why not?" I shouted, only asking because I was supposed to.

"Because I was a virgin at the time and he wanted to make me."

"Wanted to what?"

"He wanted to fuck me before we got married."

That word sounded so out of place coming from her. She was known to have walked off a set for too much frontal nudity.

Another time she refused to use the word fuck.

I needed to hear it again.

"He wanted to do what?"

"He wanted to seduce me."

"I can't hear you," I shouted over the vacuum clear.

"He wanted to fuck me."

"How strange."

"All men are alike," she said.

"Agreed. We're all horny creeps."

"But you're different, I can tell."

"You're looking for a brother?"

She laughed.

"I've learned to be very careful. That writer did not have it wrong. There really are men who will pay big money for one night with a Hollywood starlet. I could mention names, but I won't. They come from the Middle East, mostly, and most of them are like princes from Saudi Arabia. They can't have it over there, what we have to give, all that glamour and pizzazz, forbidden fruit all right, so they come here, and there is still nothing like seducing a movie star, even if it costs a million dollars, which is nothing to them, so much oil."

I wanted to know more, like whether she had ever indulged in this.

She read my mind.

"Only once," she said, and then laughed, "but not nearly for a million dollars."

With women it was always only once.

"I didn't do it for the money."

"Of course not, Katrina."

"I was born with money."

"Plus beauty."

"Thank you. I did it for the experience."

"The what?" I shouted over the vacuum cleaner.

"The experience," she shouted back.

They all did it for the experience, once.

She took me to another room, downstairs, the den, with all her trophies, the ones from ballet, modeling and beauty contests.

There were also many books in the room – Tolstoy, Dostoyevsky, Hemingway, Fitzgerald, Salinger, most prominent, and many playwrights.

Here there were no maids or vacuum cleaners.

"I see you've been reading Ionesco's *Rhinoceros.*"

"Don't you think that's the greatest play – how people can change colors one by one when a single monster arrives?"

I agreed – *to understand is to justify.*

"People are so easy to corrupt," she said. "Don't you agree?"

She kept trying to draw me into academic-speak, but I was imagining, quite vividly, what it must be like having a Hollywood movie star for free – even just once.

What would it be like to fuck a movie star? I was told that there was nothing like it in the world.

"We can't all be bought."

"You certainly can't. I was there and I saw."

"That's still open," I said.

"I don't think you'd sell your principles, Gil, but..."

She wanted to get a movie started and done on Ionesco's play – and would I be willing to direct? That, in addition to the re-make we'd been discussing.

"That would be tempting," I said.

This is what she wanted to talk to me about – not Miles Korwin?

She'd seen all my films, the documentaries, or so she said, including the one that was mentioned at CANNES, and the other one that was whispered for an Oscar, and wasn't it about time that I moved up to feature films? She had plenty of pull. She asked which director I admired most and I named a few, but mostly David Lean was my man and my inspiration.

"Aha," she said. "Zhivago."

Her father had known Pasternak, who had idolized Tolstoy. Her father was something of a Tolstoyan. The Tolstoyan Movement disdained the State (as did her father) and rejected the formalities of conventional religion. Tolstoy and his disciples imagined a world that worshipped Jesus in purity – love your enemies, depart from anger, turn the other cheek, accept no oaths.

"With my father," she said, "I once made pilgrimage to Tolstoy's home. It's been so long ago, I forget the name."

"Yasnaya Polyana," I reminded her.

She gazed up at me differently.

"Come," she said.

Chapter 12

I went to see Dr. Florence Petro as soon as I got back, well, not right away. I had to wait four more days even for an emergency appointment. The bad tooth had taken over my life. Everything got on my nerves. Music, rock, rap, hip-hop, jazz, drove me crazy, each note bonging all my teeth and going clickety-clack. Loud music hit me like a train. People bothered me when they laughed, especially that famous ear-piercing shriek, which ran through me like an electric current, and they bothered me when they shouted or when they whispered. I seemed to have grown a sixth or seventh sense. I could hear a horn honking a mile away.

I understood the language of dogs when they howled.

"Serves you right," said Dr. Petro after another set of x-rays.

I supposed it served me right when I couldn't get it up for Katrina. I simply couldn't. I couldn't get it up for the biggest star in Hollywood. I explained that it was because of the tooth and the swelling and the infection, which she could see for herself, and she agreed, ever so patiently, that that had to be the problem – and that she'd be ready any time I was ready to try her again. Very good, but meanwhile I was a disgrace to all mankind.

The real reason had to be Barbara, damn it, Barbara and only Barbara. I could only get it up for her. I was cursed. Usually what happens after a disaster like this is that the minute you leave the situation you get an erection that just won't quit, and that is exactly what happened, and I had it going even here for Dr. Petro who was quite sensational east of Hollywood.

"You simply won't listen," she said as she poked around in my mouth.

"Ouch," I said through the cotton.

"Stop complaining."

She let me know, again, that I had a very serious infection on not just one tooth but on four teeth, though one particular tooth was most troubling. I'd need an operation, oral surgery, and this was well beyond her skills. "I told you this before and I'm telling you this again. But first you have to take the pills for the infection. No dentist will do any pulling otherwise." Fact is, she said, there were gum, tissue and nerve problems associated with the teeth that were possibly beyond dentistry and that unless I got lucky, my next stop would be the hospital.

Chapter 13

Carlos Loomis had phoned me even while I was still out there in Hollywood, saying he needed me for some urgent editing.

I simply could not let him down again and I simply could not work with this problem. I'd been to another dentist who made her diagnosis complete.

I hit on something. I would offer myself as an experiment. I would find a university and sacrifice myself to those dentists in training. I'd heard about these clinics. This is where dentistry students learned their trade and where their professors were on the hunt for people like me. They'd be willing to do anything and were sure to take on hard cases.

I checked around on the Web and found dentistry hospitals all over the place, but, after the phone calls, turned out that only a few of them accepted actual patients, and those that did were not interested after I described this condition of mine. I managed to secure an appointment with a dentistry school in Brooklyn. When I showed up I found myself in a waiting room that was more like a warehouse.

There must have been 100 people packed in there in various stages of pain – adults along with their children and crying babies. My gawd! So much misery in the world! I was asked to fill out a form that ran 10 pages.

There was no place to sit. People were snaked out into the hallways. I could not concentrate for all the agony inside and out.

Turned out that this was break season for dentistry students but the professionals were in. They tended mostly to financially hardship cases.

I asked the receptionist, "How long the wait?"

"Are you kidding?" she said.

She said it was unlikely I could be seen today. "It's always like this on Monday."

How about the rest of the week?

"Not much better."

How many doctors were there for these 100 patients?

"Usually three, but Dr. Hernandez is out for the week."

I told her I had an emergency.

"Everybody has an emergency."

I kept at it for an opening. What were the chances if I came back tomorrow?

"Same as today."

She said I could always give it a try.

She said it would be better if I had false teeth. Those I could leave behind. Too bad.

On the check-in sheet I noticed that I was last, in back of the line, though soon more patients kept coming in. I imagined that these two doctors must be moving fast. Could there be time for x-rays and consultations? Most likely you walked in, got your teeth pulled, and walked out. I caught a glimpse of one of the two remaining doctors, a man likely in his 50s and exceedingly tall. He needed to check something here up front but he never gave the rest of us a look. We were livestock.

I was determined to stick it out. I filled out the paperwork and handed it over to Marcella at the desk. She found 10 spots that needed filling in. I also had to give my occupation. I was embarrassed to say filmmaker, among people who really had it bad, financially. I had written down "self-employed" but it wasn't good enough. Apparently they had to know your line of work as maybe that meant something for the doctor – logical.

So I wrote down "actor." In New York this was understood to mean that you were waiting tables.

But the crowd wasn't thinning out. I gave it six hours and then gave up.

Chapter 14

Dad insisted that there were strange goings-on here at Kessinger's. "People leave the church like zombies," he said.

He looked at Mom. "No it isn't *rapture*," he said.

I was here on a day when I caught Barbara also visiting. She had brought cakes and wine.

"They have a saint," said Dad, "and you know what her name is?"

"No, Dad, I don't."

"Saint Iris."

"So?"

"That was the name of Lot's wife."

"The one who turned to a pillar of salt," said Barbara.

"I knew that," I said.

"You've seen the statue they have right beside the church? Tell me that isn't the figure of a woman?"

"What are you trying to say, Dad?"

"This place is Sodom."

"Oh, Joseph," said Mom, nearly shrieking. "People will think you're insane."

Dad turned specifically to Barbara. "You've been to the dining room, haven't you?"

"Yes, Mr. Gilels." She would never call him Joseph or "Dad."

"Have you seen those salt shakers up and down the rows?"

She gave this some thought.

"Well what of it?" said Mom.

"They worship salt, the salt of Saint Iris."

Dad explained that back in the old days salt was the measure of a person's station in life. "Above the salt" placed you high and "below the salt" placed you low.

"Oh dear," said Mom.

Dad said that they practiced the rites of Sodom and Gomorrah, Charles Kessinger and his cult, quite the opposite of the Biblical command to pursue righteousness and justice. Here they punished kindness. Here they showed no mercy to the widow, to the orphan or to the stranger. Sodom all over again, right here in the United States.

Dad knew his Bible and quoted Ezekiel: "Pride, fullness of bread and abundance of idleness was in her and in her daughters; neither did she strengthen the hand of the poor and the needy; and she was haughty, and refrained from doing repentance before Me, and I took her away as I saw fit." He said part of it in Hebrew.

He used Biblical references frequently in his novels and reviewers sometimes punished him for such overindulgence. He read his Torah every morning before turning to his own writings. He did not pray. He did not attend religious services. He seldom participated in holy day observances. He knew some rabbis but never got along with them. But he read his Bible portion every day.

"Then again," Dad said, "why pick on Kessinger's. Sodom is all over the place. Read the headlines. We're the appetizer of what's to come and what's already done."

Mom took me aside.

"I'm worried about your father."

"It's getting worse?"

"I suppose. But he really believes all that nonsense."

"He sounds awfully lucid."

"Maybe that's the way it works?"

She started to cry.

"He waits for you all week. He wants you to get us out, as if we hadn't already tried."

Barbara and I had investigated a dozen nursing homes to get it right for my mom and dad and each one had something about it that was wrong, even sinister. By far the best choice had been this very place, Kessinger's Communal Living Estates for 55-plus. "Mayor" Kessinger himself had given us the tour. This was no nursing home. All the residents lived in bungalows, independently. Compared to the rest, this was Shangri La. (The bungalows, however, were monitored.)

But everything was controlled, even to your intake of food. Doctors' orders.

"They're starving us to death," Dad said, "to keep bringing in more customers."

The cost was $2,800 a month. But the initial payment was far greater.

"Have you ever seen such traffic?" asked Dad. "People keep moving in. We don't know what moves out, except to the graveyard."

Mom whispered that Dad had taken his cane to see how far he could get, and was stopped at the gate and escorted back quite rudely.

"Didn't Kessinger himself come in for a talk?" Dad asked Mom.

Mom didn't answer. Dad appealed to Barbara.

"He came in for the purpose of converting me."

"To what?" asked Barbara.

"To join his church."

"So what's wrong with that?" asked Mom.

"I'm expected to worship Saint Iris? The god of Sodom?"

"Maybe he meant well," said Barbara.

"They are wicked," said Dad.

For a moment I thought the hell with it all, Mom and Dad are coming home with us. I always thought that, and now more and more.

But Mom was feeble and Dad needed constant medical attention and supervision. He had blackout spells. Someone would have to stay home with him all the time.

"Have you ever asked anyone for directions since you've put us here?" Dad asked.

Dad had approved of this place at the start. In fact, he insisted on it above all the rest.

"Yes. So?"

"Is anyone ever helpful?"

I thought about this. I had to think about this.

"Barbara?"

"To tell you the truth, no," Barbara said. "Gil?"

"I guess not," I said. "But remember, most of these people are, well aged, probably hard of hearing..."

"No, they are trained to be hostile to the stranger, like Sodom."

Mom walked us to the door.

"I'll be all right," she said. "He always settles down after a tantrum."

I watched Dad get back in his chair at his desk, hitting the keys of the typewriter, just as I always remembered him.

Chapter 15

"Is there nothing to do?" asked Barbara.

We were settled in for coffee at Starbucks near her apartment on 67th and Lexington.

I had taken some pills, so the swelling was down, and I could swallow a bite or two.

"He's had two mini strokes, remember, and my mom's in no great shape, either."

"He's right, you know. People there are so unfriendly, from the help to the residents."

"What do you think of that Sodom business?" I asked.

"Your mom's right. People will think he's crazy. But he's not. He let me peek into some of the writing he's doing. He's in top form, Gil."

"I don't know what to think. Once it gets to this, nursing homes and all that – God it's depressing."

"That man Kessinger," she said. "Something about him. He's so smarmy. Do you trust him?"

"He seems to be like all those other fundamentalist types, though, it's true, who knows what god he prays to?"

"What are you saying?" she asked.

"Hell, I don't know."

"Those people, do you see how they walk? Does it give you that creepy feeling? Like Jim Jones or..."

"Stepford Wives?" I said.

"It's like they're in a daze."

"Rapture."

"You think like your dad, you know?"

"What's that mean?"

"I think you believe him."

"No. If I did I'd call the state cops. Don't forget, that place is sanctioned by the state, and the state comes around once a month for inspection."

"You think that's good enough?" she asked.

"I don't know what to think."

I was glad Barbara had been there with me and I was happy to be talking, just talking, the way we used to do. While we'd been together, as a couple, we made sure to find the time for reflection. We seldom missed dinner, unless she was teaching late, or was off on some speaking tour related to her radio show, or when I was at the track, or editing for Carlos Loomis, or making arrangements for my next documentary, or when I was driven off and forcibly detained for failure to pay off this or that gambling debt, not to mention my delinquencies with Adolf Gruberman, who liked to say "I can make accidents happen," so that in fact we often missed dinner together.

Barbara's beef was that I lacked drive and ambition and used gambling as a means to delay – delay real life and real work. I'd never convince her that there was nothing more creative than picking the right horse. It had to be love when still today, even today, even after what she had done, whether I won or whether I lost, whether it was something good or whether it was something bad, on beholding a sunrise or a rainbow, the first person I longed to share it with was Barbara. So it had to be love.

But I could not give in after what she had done, and as we shared coffee here at Starbucks after yet the most disturbing visit to my aged parents, I ran temperatures of resentment mixed with affection. At home and in public she often spoke out against people who were quick to judge. She mentioned the many public figures that had been devoured by loose lips. Recently her radio shows focused on the consequences of bullying. Those too were judgments, I agreed, when a mob picked a man out of the crowd, usually at random, and, pointing fingers, went after him.

Pointing fingers, yes, pointing fingers.

"Maybe," I said, "it's time to get them out."

"But to where?"

After Dad's most horrific fainting spell, there in the bathtub, we did in fact place him in a nursing home for full-time medical care, but only temporarily, until he got better, but he didn't get better, and he wanted no part of the place, or any place, without Mom there with him. The nurses said he kept calling out for Sylvia. Several times they had to restrain him. So we had tried that, and it didn't work. We had tried everything!

Yes, but where? *Where* was the question that haunted us.

There wasn't much to say for a while. She was all decked out. Extra rouge. Extra lipstick. Mom had whispered that she knew I was coming.

Mom had also talked about forgiveness.

"How's what's-his-name doing?" I asked.

She said nothing; kept to her coffee, or latte, or whatever.

"You know, James Headley."

"Do we have to?" she finally said.

"Did you break up with him or something?"

"Or something."

"I should know, you know. We've got divorce proceedings going on, you and me...you and me and James Headley."

"We're done, okay?"

"You're done with James? Is this what I'm hearing?"

"It was a mistake, Gil. People make mistakes."

"They sure do."

"Gee, thanks."

"Who's your next mistake? Or haven't you found one yet."

"Maybe it's you," she chuckled.

"There's more mistakes out there," I said, "just waiting for a catch like you."

"I just said..."

"I heard what you said."

"I liked making mistakes with you," she smiled.

That's one place we never failed; the bed.

Chapter 16

Playing particular numbers is always a risk. You cannot follow all the horses, all the ball games, all the lotteries. This can drive you crazy. I regretted the day that I came up with that system, which really was no system. I wish I knew what it was. I spoke to mathematicians who told me that numbers were infinite. Anything can happen. I spoke to cabbalists who told me that God created heaven and earth by uttering numbers; secret code. The letters in the Hebrew alphabet correspond to numbers.

Craps, roulette, the horses, all means of gambling are ruled by numbers, and when you shake them up, they spill out at random, which means chaos. But is it really random, or does some divine or Satanic force dictate the outcome? Even before the player rolls the dice, has the fall been predetermined? Before the horseplayer bets his choice, has the winner already been declared by a power from up above or from down below?

Is there such a thing as luck? If not, if we all make our own destiny, why do some people win and why do some people lose? I see it at the track every day. I know a man who cannot win for all the trying and I know a man who cannot lose no matter what. Gambling is a mirror for everything, for everything else, and within gambling – behold, here is the microcosm of the universe.

Every craps table is a world unto itself, from boxman, to base dealers, to stickman, and here, at the casino, I shot my numbers, and kept making my points. I had left the dentist only hours ago, got the extraction done, and was told that I needed a week's rest, but nothing could keep me from the action. I was raking it in. I ordered a drink, sipping it with the pills. My chips were riding high, all blacks.

Next I was in the infirmary. I had passed out. Security had to come and wheel me over. I was given more pills but told not to take them until the alcohol wore off. But there is nothing like a gambler in his rhythm, when he knows this is his day. That day may never come round again.

I was unsteady on my feet and the nurses gave me worried looks, but I moved on, straight to the racing room.

I had picked out the horses the night before for the late races from Santa Anita where there was a special Pick Four going on – pick four winners straight and here's the pot, half a million dollars. You had to be nuts not to get in. You could not call yourself a gambler to stay out. The jackpot was ready. The jackpot was waiting. The jackpot must not be detained.

No handicapping. I was going with luck, strictly luck, my four numbers, 4318. They corresponded exactly to the horses I liked, so that I had indeed included the element of science. But mostly luck. I bet some early races just to pass the time. I didn't expect much, though I won a few dollars. I was actually quite a big player, and became an even bigger player since I got Adolf's pot to piss in.

I still had a chunk of his money and so an average bet of mine ran somewhere between $200 and $500.

Sometimes I wagered a thousand dollars on a single race, and after you got into the habit of betting big, it was tough to go small. The racetrack, I'll say this, washed away all your troubles, or rather all your other troubles. You were on trial here, you against the odds, you against fate. The entire world was on your back, rooting against you, dumping on you, betting against you, but here you could get even. Gambling let you tell the world to go screw itself; you had your own plans. Destiny was in your hands when you palmed those dice and when you scanned the Daily Racing Form.

Compulsive? So who wasn't?

Superstitious? Who isn't? I wore my corduroy jacket for this occasion, and my blue shirt, and my dark denim pants. These always brought me luck.

Well, usually.

Bingo Freeman said, "I like my horse in the tenth."

He owned the horse, and I'll say this, he wasn't a hustler or a tout. If he liked a horse, the horse had to be a good thing.

Only in this case his horse was not my horse, the horse I had picked to finish off my Pick Four.

"But he ran sixth last time out," I said.

"He had an excuse."

He wouldn't tell what; owners and trainers and jockeys have their secrets.

I never liked getting tips. They always threw you off, off your game.

That was another reason why you did not want to make friends at the track. You did not want people giving you the kibosh, this way or that. Didn't ask. Don't tell.

The question would remain, when that race came along, how this new information would affect my betting.

Shouldn't affect it at all. Nothing happened. I didn't hear a thing.

I bet a few more of the early races and the place started filling up, and no wonder, the word was out on the Pick Four.

Smiley the Mooch came over.

"Like anything?"

"Not really," I said.

This was the last person I wanted rooting for me.

"Bingo Freeman likes his horse," Smiley said.

"Oh yeah?"

"Likes him a lot."

"Oh yeah?"

"Didn't he tell you? He told me he told you."

"I forget."

"Say, can you lend me a sawbuck? I'm running short this week and you know I always pay you back."

Smiley never pays anybody back, but I gave him $20. I always considered that charity.

"I told you that horse would win!" Smiley the Mooch shouted race after race. "I told you." But he always seemed to bet on the horse that would lose.

As the big races approached, the fire alarm went off. At first, nobody moved. The racing room and the entire casino kept going as if nothing was heard. But then came the announcement over the loudspeaker that this was no drill. Everybody must vacate the premises immediately. Now people moved fast and the room cleared out, including the tellers and No Neck, their supervisor, who ran like the chicken that he was.

I stayed. I'd heard these alarms and these messages before. Security came over and said I had to leave. He left and I didn't.

The TVs got turned off. But I stayed.

Let the place burn down, I've got races to bet. They can't do this, and usually it is a false alarm. Or a small kitchen fire. Or some idiot using the unauthorized exits, which always triggered the alarms. Back when the Garden State racetrack burned down, even as the smoke kept billowing, and even as the tellers ran off, people still tried to make their bets. That is the nature of diehards. This, though: Brinks bags with thousands of dollars in them were scattered unattended all over the floors, and at the counting later on, not a dollar was missing. Someone said, "People aren't this honest even at church."

One reason I stayed put was because I was "non-essential personnel." I always liked that, non-essential personnel. That's me.

An hour later everybody came back, essential and non-essential personnel.

The TVs came back on.

We were one race away from the start of the Pick Four at Santa Anita.

Trevor Denman, the famous Santa Anita race caller, hyped it up, and that got me even more excited.

I needed to walk off some energy so I got up and started walking around the casino. Every game was in action and the place was humming and I never felt superior to these people. I was one of them. I could think that I wasn't like them, that I wasn't as slothful as them, that I wasn't as greedy as them, that I wasn't as desperate as them, that I wasn't as gluttonous, as lustful, as envious as them, but we were all in the same boat. We all wanted that jackpot, and then all our troubles would be over.

We'd pay off all our bills. We'd tell our boss to take a hike. We'd finally take a vacation. We'd be charitable. We'd give to the poor and the needy.

We'd have buildings and chairs at universities named after ourselves.

Above all, we would chart our own course, because we had the money, and we would be masters of our own destinies because we had the money.

I placed my bets with 15 minutes to go. I added another $1,000 to win on the horse, the first horse to kick off the Pick Four. I never bet to place.

To bet place or show was cowardly. I always thought so. That was for amateurs. You liked your horse or you didn't.

If you settled for second best, that marked you as second rate.

No, there was winning and losing and nothing in between.

I used to like blackjack but unfortunately that's where amateurs often took a seat and ruined the whole game.

Amateurs ruined every game, once they showed up. They could even ruin the game of craps.

In betting the horses, it was you and you alone.

Connie Brill came over. She was one of the few women to be seen at the racing room, and more than that, she was attractive.

More than that, she liked me. I had an open invitation, but no thank you very much.

"I haven't seen you around," she said.

"I've been around," I said.

She was an advertising executive, hooked on the horses, though. I had used her for my documentary on *Protect Battered Women*.

She helped with the publicity.

"He's been asking for you," she said.

She knew Adolf Gruberman. In fact she did much of his advertising. Small world.

"I know," I said.

"Do you have something for him?"

"I've cut a couple of scenes," I told her.

"You know he'll want more."

"Of course."

"How long do you think you can keep stringing him along?"

"Until I'm done."

"Hah!"

"What?"

"I wouldn't mess with a guy like that," she said. "He knows where you spend your time, you know."

"I may never do lunch in this town again?"

"Worse."

"I hear you're getting married again, Connie," I said. "Or is it divorced?"

"A bit of both, Gil," she laughed.

"Aren't we all?"

"So I hear," she said. "How *is* Barbara?"

"We're friends."

"I always liked her. She talks about you on the radio all the time."

"Anything good?"

"You know there's always me," Connie said. "I'll take you on the rebound."

"That's a comfort."

She had just come in to bet a few horses and then leave and then check the results online. I knew (or suspected) that she was staying over and had someone in the room. She once had me upstairs with her – she was a whale, at the roulette, so everything was on the house –

and I was close to getting it done, but stopped myself when I thought of Barbara.

For some reason, the first big race seemed forever to get started. It is amazing how long it takes them to get loaded into the gate, and all that after they've been saddled in the walking ring and after they've been paraded onto the track. After all that the starters took their time getting them loaded. This seemed to take forever. Then there were always one or two horses that were fractious and acted up right at the gate.

Now there was one horse that reared up and dumped his jockey. This was never a good sign and I hoped it wasn't my horse, number four, and it was.

Finally he was in, and they were off. He was supposed to take the lead – that's how the chart showed him race for race – and sure enough he tripped at the start and got off last. Once a speedster doesn't get off it's smart to rip up your ticket. But the jockey got him settled, and relaxed, got him to change leads, moved him to cut between two rivals, and he started passing horses, and won. He won by a length.

Now I was alive for the double, the pick three and the pick four.

"Anything?" asked Smiley the Mooch.

"Nah."

"Can you spot me another sawbuck? You know I always pay you back."

I gave him another 20.

The next race, on the grass, was a head-to-head nail-bitter from start to finish, Affirmed versus Alydar all over again, and I got it by a nose.

So I had the double, which gave me a nice payoff, but now my heart started pounding for race number three toward the pick four. This third race was a laugher. My horse took the lead and never gave it up, winning by a margin of four lengths. So I had the pick three, which gave me a terrific payoff, but nothing so grand as what was coming up, if only my luck would hold.

Trevor Denman announced that the pot for the pick four had swelled to $760,000, and counting.

I had not cashed in my winnings up to this point. That could be mistaken by Fate as a wrap-up, as being done. Fate had eyes. Fate was always watching.

Over the years I had won just two pick threes, so this alone was a windfall, but I had never felt as sure as this. This cannot be explained, this feeling; a gambler's hunch can never be explained. My only concern was that on this last leg of the pick four, the horse I had going was the favorite, favorites won at a 33 percent clip, but I never did well with favorites, and besides, all the experts picked my horse, and it was Bingo Freeman's horse and I had never won on a Bingo Freeman entry. I also never won when the experts were unanimous.

So what?

I put an extra $2,000 on the horse. I wanted to pile it on. As if $760,000 wasn't enough. Greed? No. Optimism.

I walked up to the window a second time to ask Marc the teller how much Bingo Freeman had bet on his own horse.

Marc and I usually talked boxing.

Marc gave me the following figures: $10,000 to win.

This was good. This proved true confidence.

But $5,000 to place.

This was strange. Very strange.

This was weak. Very weak.

Well, this was his horse. He had to make sure against all contingencies.

But it wasn't what I had expected.

I went back and asked Marc if Bingo Freeman always or usually made place bets.

"No," he said. "He's strictly a win man, except today."

Never mind. Horses run against other horses, not against the people who bet on them. Horses can't read the tote board.

Chapter 17

I needed to take a walk before the race went off and in making the rounds throughout the casino I found myself wondering what this was all about, besides guilt, guilt about everything that I wasn't doing. I seemed to be falling behind on everything and everybody, and would even a big win make a difference? What problems would this solve? Where was I going and what was I achieving?

I had even lost touch with my dreams. I had a big car and I had a big house, so, did I need a bigger car and a bigger house?

In my documentaries, which were actually journalism put to film, I kept hoping to say something important. I had made 11 of them and I was happy with all of them, and some had been praised and had won those awards. But there was always someone else who came along and said it better, and so I always had my eye on the next project. The new technology moved so fast that there was no getting ahead of the curve, there was only the rush to do some catching up. My editing was now done digitally.

My documentary on books titled *Still Reading*? was the one that gave me a measure of fame. The question was put to high school and college students as to whether they'd still be reading paper after they graduated, as opposed to electronic books; the results were mixed. But bookstores *were* declining and, admit it or not, most re-search was being done on the Web. On reading for pleas-ure, opinions were divided. There was no firm conclu-sion, but there was no question about it, the tide had turned and a new generation was upon us.

As for my documentary on battered women, this one still got me hate mail. This one took me into territories I could not have imagined, not only for the severity but also for the numbers. So many of our women were get-ting hurt by brutish husbands that, as presented in the documentary, experts could only declare it a national dis-grace and a national emergency. This was an epidemic. It was worse overseas, in parts of the Middle East and parts of Africa, but that was no comfort.

I had covered the rape case in India, and indeed the rape *epidemic* in India, and was surprised what came out of the interviews with "the man on the street." I was there, on the spot reporting, to hear men say that wom-en were asking for it and that a woman's place was in the home and whatever else she got she deserved. Some laughed at the predicament being faced by a woman who had been brutalized on a bus. This had made the headlines, had even gotten me on the BBC, so I reported on it, did a quick documentary on it, but would anything change?

Can anything change human nature – or was it cul-ture?

But the one that beat them all, I supposed, was on *Hitler's Conductor*, Wilhelm Furtwangler. This was like-wise my favorite because it featured the classic moral dilemma and asked the age-old question – what would you do if you were in his shoes? That was Barbara, back when she was mine and mine alone, who had dared me to do this, and I did. I had no regrets, despite the firestorm that came thereafter.

I was wary on something so touchy to my father and his generation.

I was worried about getting the perfect voice for such a job. "You've got to do this," Barbara had insisted.

I did not want to come off as an apologist.

Furtwangler was not Hitler's Conductor. That was the accusation and after the war he stood trial and was exonerated. But the stigma never left and performers like Horowitz shunned him, as did Toscanini, but that was pure jealously. Herbert Van Karajan was the true Nazi. He joined the party twice! Furtwangler never joined it once. He saved people who played with him for the Berlin Philharmonic. They idolized him. All of Berlin did, all of Germany, all of America, in parts.

Hitler idolized him. Furtwangler refused to shake hands with him, Furtwangler refused Hitler, risking his life for that snub, so Hitler ran up on stage, grabbed his hand for a handshake, pictures were taken, circulated around the world, and the image stuck. Poor Furtwangler. He was encircled coming and going, but he could have left the country, and he didn't.

He argued that he was a musician and that art and politics should not mix and, more than that, art should elevate the culture, in his case, the Third Reich culture. He thought he could make a difference and of course he couldn't, he was being used to present the world a false face. He was naïve and he was also German, Beethoven's kind of German.

So why didn't he leave? Wouldn't that have been heroic?

"No," said Barbara, always heated on the subject. "To stay was heroic, to stay and save his orchestra. He saved a hundred lives."

"Books have been written on this," I argued. "Movies have been made."

"Not like you can do."

"This would take time. Five years of research."

"There are still survivors. Leave it to me to find them."

It irked her that Van Karajan reaped all the glory. After the war, and after his death, his estate was worth $50 million, or maybe it was $500 million.

Furtwangler died in disgrace and in shame. He continued to conduct but always with that stain.

True, what would I have done in his shoes? That's what I kept asking myself whenever Barbara got it going on this.

People told me there'd be trouble if I went ahead with this, but I was always a sucker for moral dilemmas. We faced them every day.

Some big. Some small. Furtwangler faced impossible choices whichever way he turned. I had focused on the man and his times.

We can't go around judging people when we don't have the facts and the circumstances – and even when we do. My favorite line came from Philo: "Be kind. For everyone you meet is fighting a great battle." I had started to sketch something out for a documentary on Furtwangler – placing him counterpoint against Van Karajan for the purpose of dramatic conflict – and each time I got to studying what went on at that time I started to get depressed and confounded, but I persisted.

I didn't know what I would do, but I kept siding with Furtwangler, and this worried me. He did perform for

Hitler. That's even on YouTube. But he also wrote a letter to Goebbels, telling him off. That took guts. What would I do if I was made head of the Jewish Council, say in the Warsaw Ghetto, and had to snitch on my neighbors, inform on them, denounce them, betray them – lie after lie?

Would I do that? No. But would I do that to save my own wife and kids? Now we're facing Sophie's Choice.

The Nazis did that all the time. I didn't need that from the books. My father told me. He had an older sister who died in Auschwitz. She had twins. The Gestapo showed her two trains. One was going to Treblinka. The other was going to Paris and freedom. She had to make a choice on the spot. It was up to her, on a whim, if her kids were to live or die. She pointed to *that* train, never to know what happened, but tortured by the thought that she had doomed her kids – unaware that both trains were destined for Treblinka.

Who would want to be in those shoes?

I was too thoroughly American – too accustomed to my pleasures – to understand any of this. People were old but were still alive to have endured this.

So this wasn't history. Not yet. This happened only a moment ago (in the clock of history).

"We're awfully spoiled," Barbara had said.

Barbara had a bleeding heart. There was no sense talking politics with her. She got too emotional and got everybody else all riled up. She wanted to "repair the world" and she would do so singlehandedly if she had to. On her radio show and on her blogs she shared her opinions with thousands, inviting hate mail in return, and she could bang out a dozen letters to the editor in one sitting.

She wanted justice. Opinions varied on justice. Her latest campaign was on a biography that had come out from a woman who had claimed (and don't they all?) that she had slept with JFK. She described him, John F. Kennedy, as a horn-dog and a sleaze. Barbara was furious. "Maybe it's true and maybe it isn't. But anybody can say anything about anybody – especially when they're dead."

"But you had me do Furtwangler."

"To do him justice. To *undo* a wrong."

Books were coming out on other celebrities (mostly dead) and it was all about depravity.

Barbara was right. Anybody can say anything about anybody.

This was the age of gossip and reality TV. Everybody wanted to get into the act. Filmmakers had to compete with all that noise. We were competing against walking telephones that could take pictures on the run, and make movies that turned everyone into an actor and a director. We had company. We were not alone. Amateur hour.

This one, Furtwangler, got awful reviews. But in making it I kept wondering how we would react if we were ever taken over by a tyrant. That's why it was important and that is why I didn't mind the avalanche of bad reviews – and I wish that were the truth. Bad reviews always seem unjust and unfair, and they always hurt, especially when your critics misunderstood you through ignorance or baseless hatred. One line from a critic could doom two years of blood, sweat and tears.

What if a Joseph McCarthy became president?

What if, to save our own skins, we were commanded to snitch on co-workers, acquaintances, neighbors, even friends, even family members?

Chapter 18

For some reason it came to me, the remembrance of the first time we met. Barbara was still at work at that advertising agency (as senior vice president) and I had come in – into her private office – to ask questions about one of their clients, a university, that was in hot water over a course that was being given on masturbation. Her job was to explain to the world why this wasn't ridiculous. My job was to get the story. I had a crush on her from the start; from the moment I walked in and beheld this beauty so reserved, so delicate and so Bryn Mawr.

We got to talking about this and that, and for the purpose of my interview, I asked her if she ever indulged.

"I beg your pardon?" she said.

"Well, yes," I said, "since this seems to be the trend, do you ever do this?"

"What a question," she said.

"So what's the answer?"

She said that she had tried it once, or twice, but that it did not work for her, since she was not a "sexual being" and seldom got "turned on."

"But it is getting awfully hot in here," she added with a smile, her features getting all flushed up.

For some reason I felt that I had gotten to her. There was going to be action between us.

So prim and proper – and that made it all the more delicious, just getting her to squirm.

"That sounds awful," I said.

"What does?" she asked, beginning to smile and continuing to squirm.

"It must be awful being so sexless."

"Well I'm not frigid or anything like that," she said. "I just don't get turned on, not very easily."

"But you're not frigid."

"NO!"

"But you just don't get turned on."

"Not like other women do," she said softly and beginning to wear down. "Why is it so hot in here?" She started fanning herself.

I wanted her this moment.

"So if I were to kiss you, you wouldn't feel a thing," I said.

"Kiss me?"

"Kiss you."

"When?"

"Now."

"Where?"

"Right here," I said.

"Impossible," she said.

"Why?"

"People might come in," she said.

That was the only drawback?

I checked outside into the hallways. It was lunchtime.

"There's nobody out there," I said.

"Well maybe some other time," she said, getting up to walk me to the door and dismiss me.

But I knew that I had her.

"As an experiment," I said, as I grabbed her gently but firmly by the arms and twirled her against the wall right next to the door before she could get it open. If she resisted, I didn't notice, and, it seemed, neither did she. I ran my palms carefully down her blouse as I had her against the wall. She whimpered when I got to her nipples underneath her bra and began toying with them and then stopped toying and took her breasts fully in a furious sexual massage. She was beginning to breathe heavily, and for a moment pushed me back, in an unconvincing gesture.

I had her top off, along with the bra. I had her half naked. There'd be no going back. I had established territorial rights.

I could do whatever I wanted with her – if the kiss would work. We both knew it without a word, despite her timid resistance.

"We can't do this," she finally said, turning away.

I spun her back. I kissed her softly. She began to purr. Then I kissed her hard. Her breathing came fast.

"Spread your legs," I whispered.

She did so, obediently, and I reached under her skirt, found the spot, and massaged, and she moaned, and lost control. She climaxed.

I left, went to the drugstore and came back. She was arranging something along a file cabinet.

"I can't seem to find that file," she said without looking up at me, but not surprised at seeing me back so soon. She'd been expecting me.

She was pretending to be busy with work, but I knew she had something else on her mind.

"You brought something?" she said laughing nervously.

I said nothing. To say anything would spoil the moment. A wrong word from me or from her could set off different vibrations, and she knew this.

There was no question that she knew this, even as she occasionally, from this moment of fury to that, offered some form of protest.

She knew, as I did, that nothing could make us stop. We both knew it from the moment of that kiss, when her knees buckled. We knew it when she let me undo her blouse with such ease, and when she even helped, if reluctantly, and still under protest – when she helped me undo her bra. We knew it when her breathing turned erratic when I began toying with her strawberry nipples...and when I reached down underneath and got busy between her legs with only mild resistance. We both knew it when she began heaving and panting.

She had spread her legs at first asking. She had said, "You don't know what those words do to a woman."

Even a woman who never gets turned on?

I gave her every chance to break loose, but she continued to submit. The path to the door was always open, but she stayed, with only mild protestations. She was only worried that someone might come in, but then she stopped worrying about that and everything else.

Now, coming back, I turned her up to her desk. She steadied herself along the edge of the desk, her back turned to me. She knew what was coming.

She wanted this as much as I did, this woman who had declared herself near sexless.

She was ready. She turned and offered an over-the-shoulder smile. That smile, coming from where it did, drove me crazy.

I was insane with heat for her. I had never felt this sensation, never before. Never like this.

Her being so refined and demure had driven me to the need to corrupt her. I needed to finish her off, properly, and she wanted it done.

She'd play it reserved, as all the while she kept giving in.

I lifted her skirt, pulled down her panties, and worked myself in. She was tight and being uncooperative, but soon she got the idea and began working with me, began understanding the rhythm and finding the rhythm, pushing back and riding forth to a beat that we arrived at together, and rotating her ass, nearly in circles, and finally we began teaming together. We worked beautifully together and once in a while I tucked my fingers in and this led to further groans of ecstasy.

She directed me to other spots where she wanted to be massaged – but never breaking stride.

"There?" I said.

"Yes."

"That's good," she said. "That's so good."

"Faster?"

"Okay."

I began using the fast and slow strategy.

"Which do you like better?" I asked.

"Just keep doing what you're doing," she said, throwing me another over-the-shoulder smile, breathing hard, her face bathed in red heat.

I began teasing her. I pulled out.

"Enough?" I said.

"No," she yelled.

"More?"

"Yes, more!"

I stroked fully.

"Like that," she said. "Like that," she said.

"Say please," I said.

"No," she said.

"Say please," I said. "Or I stop."

"Don't stop."

"Say please."

"No."

So I stopped.

"Please," she said.

"That's better."

Then I stopped again.

"Are you done?" she asked.

"What's my name?"

"What's your name?"

"What's my name?"

"Gil Gilels," she said.

"I want you to beg," I said as I inserted myself partly and stroked gently.

"That's good," she said. "Oh that's good. Please don't stop."

Not bad for someone who doesn't get turned on.

"Now beg," I said as I took a break.

"I said PLEASE didn't I?"

"Now beg," I said as I withdrew completely.

"I'm begging. I'm begging."

"Okay."

"Like that," she said. "Just like that, please, please. Yes, yes, yes, oh gawd yes."

She came again, but I hadn't. No, I wanted to save this.

Was it the same day or another day when she said, "What about you?"

She was seated at her desk. She was no virgin but she had never seen it or touched it close up. I had her open her blouse to show one nipple, for some reason one nipple and one nipple only. She unzipped me. She said, "It's so hard." I said it was all her fault. She asked if it was okay to stroke it and I said okay. She began stroking, hard, and asked if she was doing it right and I said she could vary the rhythm, so she slowed it down.

"Like this?" she said.

"Like that," I said.

She did this as she glanced up at me with happy and naughty eyes, and she kept at it with no thought of stopping.

"Am I hurting it?" she asked.

"No," I said.

"I like doing this," she said.

She must have done this before. She acted like it was her first time. Maybe it was. She was an amateur at this, and that made it all the better.

"Can I kiss it?" she asked.

"Please."

She kissed it and went back to stroking.

"Should I put it in my mouth?"

"Yes."

That's when she really went to town.

This was a socialite doing this.

"What's better?" she asked. "In my mouth or with my hands?"

I laughed. "Is this a test?"

She didn't laugh. She was too busy.

"You can do both together," I said.

She learned to alternate, as if it were a new discovery.

"What happens when you come?" she asked, using both hand and mouth in tandem.

"I don't know."

"Should I keep doing it?" she asked.

"Do you want to?"

"Yes."

I had enough of this, lifted her off her chair, and began turning her around, leaning her back against the desk.

"No," she said. "This time from the front. I want to see your face."

"Later," I said.

For some reason I wanted her from behind.

She phoned me later that night to say that she had masturbated and had climaxed six times, and now we had a routine, once a week, in her office, that's where she wanted it, in her office; later perhaps, we would do it at my place or her place – or get a room. She didn't want to fall in love. She wanted conversation kept to a minimum. There'd be no lunches, no dinners, no birthdays to keep, no anniversaries to remember, no gifts to get or to receive, no plans to be made for the future. There were to be no questions about who else we're seeing. There would only be the sex and that should keep us both happy enough. She was twenty-eight and had a career and nothing but a career to pursue. "You'll be my stud," she said cheerfully.

Meanwhile she showed up on Page Six and even in *The New York Times* linked to this or that most eligible bachelor and for some time I was all right with the arrangement, but then got fed up. When I failed to keep my appointment she waited two weeks before phoning to ask what was going on. I told her that I was tired of the deal. The sex was good, yes, the sex was terrific, the sex was sensational, but it wasn't enough.

There was more that I didn't mention. I had become jealous. What was she doing with those "eligible bachelors" she was seeing and who was that on the phone?

She could talk for hours and never stop laughing and when I arrived the phone took precedence.

We met for lunch.

"I don't have time to fall in love," she said.

"I'm pretty busy myself," I said.

"I'm having no other affairs," she said, "if that's what you're thinking. Are you?"

"No."

"That's not what I hear," she said.

I also made Page Six.

"There's nothing going on," I said, which was true. Who had the energy?

"I worry that in your business there's so much temptation."

"That's Hollywood," I said.

"But you're in that business."

"I'm a journalist, Barbara."

"But you're surrounded by actors."

"Most of them are real people," I said.

There was a long pause.

"But we're doing so well as we are," she said.

"That can't go on."

"Do you love me?" she said, and now, now in this crazy moment, she began to weep.

"Yes."

"I love you, Gil, and I was afraid this was going to happen. I didn't want it to happen, but it did. I am in love with you."

Chapter 19

I was flooded with all those thoughts as I waited for the official result of the final race of my pick four. The jackpot had reached $820,000 and my horse had finished first. There was no doubt about it – my horse had finished first, but the results were not up yet, making it official, and there was never money to be counted until the sign went up. Anything could still happen.

I had big plans for that money. First on the agenda was to pay off Adolf Gruberman and be done with him and quit looking behind my back and quit feeling guilty about taking all that money under false pretenses, as I had absolutely no intention of making that anti-Semitic film. How had I ever gotten myself into this pickle? Well, I needed the money. I was being hounded for some money that I owed, I was actually being threatened by some of the big boys, for gambling debts, and I heard that there was this guy in search of a filmmaker for a particular film. Somehow we met and I was only half listening to what the project was about. My mind was hard on the money.

I was only thinking of the money to square off my debts, never thinking that I would have to really make this documentary. I also thought that no one could be *that* unreasonable, that when it got down to the work he would have to understand that both sides of the story would have to be told – though I never intended to do that, either. My point of view was strictly on the side of the Israelis, the Jews altogether.

My gawd, they invented the medicines against polio. Adolf and the rest of them were walking around instead of being pushed around on wheelchairs strictly because of Salk and Sabin and more medical and technological advances, including cell phones, kept coming out from Israel. The journalist Jay Garfield, my friend and my political conscience, the man who ran the *Manhattan Independent*, wanted me to go ahead with a documentary on a topic that was personally precious to him. Muslims accounted for 20 percent of the world's population, and in the course of more than 100 years had produced 10 Nobel Prize winners. Jews, accounting for 0.2 percent of the world's population, and within the fields of medicine, economics, physics, peace and literature – Jews, inside of Israel and out – had produced 181 Nobel Prize winners. Where was that story?

But Jay Garfield did not have that kind of money; Adolf Gruberman's kind of money.

Back in Germany in the late 1800s Europe, Dr. Paul Ehrlich found his "magic bullet" that turned out to be the first effective treatment against syphilis. Here was another Nobel Prize winner, Jewish, so do that story, and ask what the world would be like if Einstein and Freud and so many others like them had been trapped in Hitler's Europe. Do that documentary into teeth of a world that seeks to isolate the Jewish state through sanctions and boycotts – and Jay Garfield, just like me, wasn't even Jewish.

Cures for cancer were right around the corner throughout Europe in the mid to late 1800s and into the 1900s, and especially in the 1930s, thousands of researchers, particularly on immunology, were closing in on defeating the disease, but those were the days of intolerance uber alles, so it all ended up in the chimneys of Auschwitz, the men and the women along with their remedies, up in smoke.

Jay Garfield, quite a character, and also addicted to gambling. Yes, they walked among us, and yes, they will always be with us, and as I was taught that one time I attended that GA meeting, there is no such thing as a casual gambler or an occasional gambler. Once you made your first bet or bought your first lottery ticket, welcome to the fraternity – you were a gambler, period, compulsive, addicted.

There were millions of stories about people who had lost their entire life's savings through gambling, and sometimes it was no more professional and sophisticated than driving up the corner to the convenience store to stack up on lottery tickets – and who was encouraging this? State governments from coast to coast. They ran ads encouraging people to gamble. Incredible!

Professionals like Jay Garfield and me were down on lotteries, because there was no wisdom involved, just sheer luck. But we indulged because there they were, those lottery tickets, all decked out in different colors to entice you to take the plunge, just as those liquor bottles in bars were designed and arranged so artfully for the alcoholic. As for the lottery winners who hit it really big, like $200 million, their stories usually did not end well. Nobody can have it all. There is always a price to pay. There are no happy endings for winners and losers.

He was a powerful editor of a powerful newspaper, Jay Garfield. He used to see both sides of a story, as he had to, as editor in chief, but he gradually changed, and I do not know what snapped him into a sage-like crusader against injustice, but something happened and though he kept his front pages impartial, his editorials turned dark, fearful of a world gone mad, mad with hatred. It may have happened when one of his staffers got raped in Egypt.

Jay was my hero and whatever distressed him, distressed me. One of his reporters had been kidnapped in Gaza, and was still being held captive. Jay was in love with one of his staffers, his book page editor, Lyla, only she was married, and married to another staffer who had converted to Islam, so it all got quite political and ugly. So there he was, in the middle of a love triangle, and he couldn't get out. His predicament was fodder for Internet gossip. I told him he was stupid for getting involved like this until I remembered my own situation.

We really are pushovers when it comes to women – and why is it that for so many of us the right woman comes along only *after* we've been married?

Not so with me, but that *is* the case generally, for some reason.

A man who would be king in England gave it all up for the love of a woman. Figure that out.

Maybe, I was thinking, there was a Plan B for my mom and dad and whatever the cost, I would have the money and I would get it done. I had already done some checking and found that there were places in Florida that were true resorts for the aged – except for the fact that I'd been turned down when I mentioned their medical conditions. You had to be in good health and I had to tell the truth.

Would I even consider taking that job in Hollywood? Now with my riches I would have the leverage to demand my own casting. They knew when they were talking power to power. They knew they had you when you were in no position to finagle, and that is when they set the terms and treated you like the family's poor relative. That would not be the case this time. Soon I would call the shots.

Chapter 20

This can drive you crazy, waiting for the results to be made official up on the tote board. I saw Bingo Freeman pacing up and down, his eyes darting up at the TV screen every other second for the OFFICIAL posting. He only owned the horse. I had a fortune waiting to get collected up at the window. Marc, the teller who sold me the ticket, kept glancing my way with worried looks. He was in line for a whopper of a tip from me. Would $1,000 be okay? I was usually quite generous when I was flush with cash.

Of all the tellers, he was the only one who smiled for the customers, for the players. I guess they looked down on us, as degenerates, so what were they doing here? Or maybe they had their own troubles. I keep going back to Philo when he said, "Be kind, for everyone you meet is fighting a great battle." I guess that's true, and maybe that's why people have become so unfriendly these last few decades, in general. Maybe that's a big city thing and maybe out in small-town America it's different.

Bingo Freeman made his money "social networking" and I guess that meant something like Facebook. He owned about a dozen horses and this one, the one we were waiting to be declared the winner officially – he had won by a length – this one was a three-year-old stakes-bred, so he was eligible for the Kentucky Derby if his earnings were big enough, a double reason for Bingo's anxiety. The results were still not up.

I failed to understand Facebook – how it is possible for people to have 50,000 friends? Most people, in real life, were lucky to have five.

Once I collected my winnings, I wondered if I should take a limo back. Why not? I may need Security. The money, for that amount, would be paid by check. Taxes, state and local, would have to be taken out. That would leave me with around $600,000; not bad, either. That still counts as a life-changing event. Maybe I'd hire a full-time chauffeur to drive me around. Maybe this, maybe that, but still waiting.

Bingo Freeman came over to me and said, "I don't know what to think. What do you think?"

"I don't know," I said. "What do you think?"

"I don't know," he said.

"It is taking an awfully long time," I said.

A couple of ladies who had wandered in, refugees from their slot play, had two dollars to win on the horse that had finished second.

They had shrieked when it got close to the wire – and that was their bet, two dollars.

Freddie came over and said, "This is taking a long time."

He was an engineer. He did not consider himself compulsive or even a gambler though he was here whenever I was around. He bet for the love of the math.

Everybody had a reason. Forty million of us had reasons.

The sign went up. Finally, something.

Only this: There was both an Inquiry and an Objection – against the winner, my horse, my $800,000.

If that horse got taken down, everything was lost. That was a big IF. They started showing the replay as it had been played back to the stewards and there had indeed been bumping in the stretch by the top two horses – only whose fault? My horse had been tight along the rail, with the lead, but his rival kept at him as if to squeeze him, so my jockey kept whipping his horse left-handed, causing him to drift out and impede the path of his rival.

Could go either way. My jockey was probably on the phone to the stewards protesting that he was being squeezed and had no choice but to whip left-handed. It was the other rider's fault, and the other rider would probably be on the phone to say that his lane had been interfered. So now it was up to the stewards. There was seldom a change in results in stakes races such as this one, unless the infraction was really gross and unforgivable. But you never knew. This too was random. This too was luck. We were at the mercy of randomness and luck and you did not need to be a gambler to know this.

The two ladies who had two dollars on the second horse shrieked again when the Inquiry and Objection sign went up.

If the results were overturned they would double their money and might collect $6.

Happy days.

I was annoyed at this shrill of their voices and I was annoyed at everything. What were the odds against winning and then losing all in the same race? Rich man, poor man. During the actual race, live, it was a sight beautiful to behold. My horse took the lead from the rail easy as can be and the rider had him coasting along at slow fractions so that he'd have plenty left at the finish.

There was no one even close. He had the track to himself and would have to fall apart completely to get caught. But you never counted your money until it was over. Then came the challenge, but my horse dug in, and they kept going at it as meanwhile my horse never gave up the lead. He was never headed – not even at the wire. I did not yell, I did not whoop, for this was not my style. I never showed whether I had won or lost. I kept a poker face. Even this time, with $800,000 on the ride.

I saw no infraction, no foul, but I knew, again, never to count yourself the winner until the results were official, and even then there was concern as to whether you had the right ticket. This also happens; with so many racetracks you could bet the wrong track and it happened to me before and it happens to everybody. Some people were so lucky that *because* they bought the wrong ticket for the wrong track, they ended up winning. That never happened to me.

So here I kept checking my ticket and yes, everything was correct.

Pastor Reickart was here and I wondered who he was praying for.

There really is no choice except to stick it out and accept your medicine if it comes to that, take it like a man, take it like a pro. There is no one around to feel sorry for you and there was no one to even hear your story. Everybody has a story and this? – another day at the races. Tell people your story and they'll say, "You think that's something? Wait till you hear this."

This is true even in the arts where it was each man for himself and no matter what you did, how many years of suffering you put in, the glory comes and goes, if there is glory at all. Really, it is astonishing how it is when your masterpiece is acclaimed one minute and vanishes the next, two to four years of hard labor over a book, a scoop, a painting, a symphony, a movie, all disappear without a trace. There is no one to talk to about that, either. People are busy. People have their own lives. If you failed, you failed, and if you succeeded, very good, congratulations, but it is all so fleeting.

This could be a disaster. Do you pray? No, God doesn't even want you in a place like this. He doesn't visit the casinos and he hears no prayers from gamblers. He had other business and he would laugh if you mentioned the word disaster in connection with your loss, even at $800,000. You want disaster? I will give you disaster. You want pity? Let me take you for a tour around the world, or never mind that, visit your neighborhood hospital. Visit the sick, visit the poor, visit the needy, and then tell men how you're hurting. I gave you Hurricane Sandy. Need I say more? In Staten Island they're still living in tents – and how about that Tsunami I gave Japan? Would you like a taste of that, you and your troubles at the racetrack? I created horses to plow, not to race.

I left for another smoke down the other end of the casino where smoking was permitted. This was no time to light up a cigar, but I lit one up anyway just for a few puffs. There was a man sitting at a machine drinking beer from an expensive bottle, I couldn't make out the brand and besides, I didn't drink beer and never cared much for beer. "You're not going to smoke that here?" the man said.

"Huh?"

"Get out of here with that," he said.

Now what to do? Just leave? Isn't this like road rage? You just drive on. You don't know them and they don't know you. It is not personal.

One road rage incident can change your entire life.

So it is best to move on.

But I was angry.

"You see the sign?" I said.

"Yeah I see the sign."

"The sign says smoking permitted."

"I can read asshole. But you can't smoke cigars."

"Where does it say that?" I asked.

"Just move."

"I don't think so."

"That cigar stinks."

"Beer smells terrific," I said, "like piss. All that farting, all that burping, all that from you and your beer."

He got up to face me. Just lay a hand on me. Be the first. The eye in the sky would catch any action.

But I felt silly and I was glad when he sat back down without a word.

I went back to the racing room.

In a stricken state we all kept staring at the TV tote board waiting for the results to change or stay. My mouth was dry. I could hear my heart pounding. Was I getting lightheaded? Were the dizzy spells coming back? I bit down on a piece of ice and now another tooth started going bad. Me and my teeth. Cursed on that score, heredity from my father. I had spent $32,000 dollars getting him implants. We all thought he still had a healthy life to live. Who knew it would all fall apart, and so fast?

But wasn't it a beautiful sight watching my horse go wire to wire? My GAWD I had the winner and $800,000, or however it would be divided up. Would I ever come back to the races if the worst were to happen? How could I? How could I not? How many times had I sworn off the races only to return as if nothing had happened? Everybody said that – "I'm never coming back."

I took out my Kindle to do something, anything, and started reading Salinger's *The Catcher in the Rye* but it was Salinger himself who always intrigued me. Here was another obsessive/compulsive, only with him it was about writing, as it was about Bobby Fischer, only for him it was about chess, but we were all in the same boat, ruthless in our singular pursuit. I was doing what they did, only my artistry was different.

A bag lady started making the rounds for handouts. I did not want her approaching me. I did not want her curses. She had the evil eye. I did not want to exchange glances accidentally or on purpose. I had seen her around. She was here often, as many times as Security dumped her back onto the streets. She had the evil eye, all right, and if you gave her nothing or if you gave her something it was never enough, and she gave you the evil eye. Bad timing for this.

I lowered my eyes deep into my racing book hoping she would pass over me, but here she was.

"Excuse me, sir..."

"I'm sorry," I said, because to have anything to do with her, good or bad, was to invite her wrath.

"I'm sorry, too," she harped, and left, but I shuddered.

Who asked for her? Who sent for her? Whose game was this? There is no trifling the power of a curse. Strange powers are at work. Judgments are being made. Iniquities are being weighed. Tribunals are in session. Witnesses are being heard and cross-examined. Prosecutors are making the case. The jury sits rapt and grim.

The angels are voting!

Smiley the Mooch came over.

"If you got the top horse you got it in the bag."

That son of a bitch, a case where a blessing was a curse. He was sure to give it the kibosh.

"You got it?" Smiley asked.

"Smiley, please, not now."

"You got the horse, I know you do."

"Please."

"Did you play the pick four?"

People shouted at the TV tote board, "Stay."

"Take it down."

"Stay."

Arguments broke out.

"That horse interfered."

"He didn't touch nobody."

"You seen what I seen?"

"Yeah, he was clear."

"He smothered the whole field."

"You don't know what you're talking about."

I asked Black Dude Andre what he saw.

"I saw nothing worthy of a change," he said. "It all depends on who the stewards put their money on."

"You still believe that?" I said.

"Hey, Gil, do you know me?"

"Yes I know you."

"Have you ever known me to believe in *anything*?"

"It's all rigged, right."

"You doubting the Big Bopper, man? Who the Big Bopper?"

"You the Big Bopper."

"Got that right," he said.

There was pushing and shoving. Security came by and said to pipe down. I was calm. I was resigned. Expect the worst, always. That is playing it safe, at least. You can't fall when you're already down. I went back to my Kindle and read Knute Hamsun's *Hunger*. This boy could write until he got off the reservation and fell in with the wrong crowd, but still a remarkable read, Kafkaesque before Kafka. Kafka saw it all coming, as did Orwell and Beckett and Ionesco, a world that was seduced into self-ishness and that succumbed to bureaucracy and to the lure of brute force and mindlessness.

They wrote their prose in plain English, or plain whatever. But they kept it sublimely simple, like Hemingway and James M. Cain and Salinger. I sought filmable language that cut the crap and the bullshit. I wrote my scripts and directed my documentaries with them in mind, asking myself, would they approve? I'd call myself a disciple of Albert Maysles, the godfather of my trade; best known for *Grey Gardens, Gimme Shelter* and *Salesman.* But mostly I saved myself for Charles Bukowski. Would he approve?

James M. Cain wrote the near perfect novel; *The Postman Always Rings Twice.* That was required reading when I taught documentary filmmaking.

Learn this to say it straight and simple. Depart from embellishments. Don't get smart. Don't explain. Assume that your viewers (or readers) already know.

People are already ahead of you. Surprise them by being straightforward.

Don't leave the people with answers. Leave them with questions.

Does it matter if the words and pictures are pretty?

"I have the second horse," said Smiley.

That was a good sign. The racing gods never favored Smiley and his kind.

Bets were made as to whether there would be a change in the results; side bets. More side bets were made as to how many more minutes it would take.

Gamblers – we even bet on the weather.

What company I keep!

I was surprised at finding myself so uninterested and so passive. Had I gained wisdom with age and experience? Had I learned to see the Big Picture? Had I finally become smart? Smart – this was what horsemen called aging racehorses that refused to leave the starting gate. They were wised up to the routine. They were tired, raced-out and had enough. This? This was small stuff. How ridiculous to care.

Finally, here it came, and the news was not good.

Chapter 21

Adolf Gruberman showed up again in Greenwich Village. He had got the legalities untangled so that Carlos Loomis could get back to work on the streets. He had only stopped it to prove what he could do when displeased, as he was displeased with me. I wanted to see him anyway. Some strangeness here as it appeared that Carlos and Adolf were getting along, which could only mean that they were teaming up against me. Or maybe I was being paranoid. But it was strange.

I saw them whispering and smiling and backslapping. Maybe he had Carlos in mind for his next documentary. Or *this* documentary?

The one I was working on, or rather the one I was not working on.

Carlos – I'd been back to work a week – had been friendly to me as well, which made me suspicious. I knew a false front when I saw one.

"Here's your man," Carlos said when I was in the middle of a shoot.

"My man?"

"My mistake," Carlos said.

I had grown to dislike Carlos. He had no warmth, no personality, neither for me, nor for the rest of the crew.

He was all business like David Lean but he was no David Lean and he sure was no Albert Maysles.

When I first met him I asked if he had seen my work. "Yes," he had said, with no further comment.

I hated it when people did that...and they knew exactly what they were doing.

That is spitefulness.

Adolf had been emailing me throughout and I'd been ignoring his messages and he had grown to expect my delinquencies. Most disturbing about Adolf Gruberman was that he was not all bad. He could not be dismissed. He belonged to library and hospital boards. He had a soft spot for liberal causes. He ran campaigns in support of undocumented workers and backed it up with money. He was a money-bags advocate for literacy and returning veterans' rehab programs...just when you thought you had someone figured out.

All the same, he could be tough and hateful. He ran with that crowd of idealists, people who wanted to "repair the world" and who despised you if you disagreed with them on global warming/climate change or whatever else they had on their agenda "to make the world a better place." He used his newspapers to slander anyone with an opposing point of view. I once told him that the first people who needed repairing were idealists for being so in love with themselves that they had no tolerance for their neighbors. First repair yourself, then the world. Use that as a first step.

That crowd of his danced to every step of the far left. They had no questions, only answers. They had certainties and no doubts. They were against bullying and hate crimes though they knew how to bully and they sure knew how to hate without calling it a crime. On 9/11, they believed we brought it upon ourselves. We deserved what we got.

As for me, I could find no place for either extreme.

Adolf did enough good works to keep him on TV, and when he appeared it was never in a debate with some other guest. He had it all to himself.

He was a powerful man. His lawyers wrote constitutions for emerging countries.

He invited me to his home. I declined. I knew that would involve all that business with his daughter Helen.

"Would you rather we meet at Aqueduct?" he said.

I caught the dig. I wasn't there in the room when my horse was taken down. I had left, deciding that whatever will be will be and that I'd learn what happened on my iPhone along the Web. I couldn't bear people screaming against my horse if the worst happened. What you never wanted was to be around ladies screaming over the $6 they had won. That would make it all the more devastating, the sound of those voices.

Was that my worst day at the races? Probably, but there had been so many other bad days – who knew?

But this was a tough one to get over and that's when you begin to wonder if all your luck was turning in that direction. After all, gambling *was* a microcosm of life itself and if the dice landed properly and if the horses ran true, luck was in your favor all around...but if you sevened-out and kept getting beat by a nose, you knew it was time to watch your step, nothing was going to work out.

I had no proof of this, but it was what I believed. I still believed in the power of numbers. How was it that 7 and 11 so often went together? If you were betting an exacta and you liked the 7 horse, you had to tie it up with the 11, even if the 11 was 99 to 1. Would Mickey Mantle be the same without his number 7 and would Bobby Orr be the same without his number 4 and would

Maurice Rocket Richard be the same without his number 9?

I had never been so close, nothing that close that I could recall. I had a fortune right in my hands, and it slipped away.

The angels had voted against me.

Were we really being maneuvered? Was everything preordained? What is this about free will when some people had all the luck?

I knew people who worked hard all their lives and got nothing in return. I met them in the unemployment lines. I'd had those years as well, when there were no takers for my documentaries and there was no money coming in. Fortunately I had built an archive with the newspaper so that I was eligible, and there I was, with the rest of the unemployed, waiting in line, and you were always waiting in the wrong line. You had the wrong papers. You had to go back and start all over again. The clerks disdained you. You were livestock to be branded.

I knew days when there was no food. I knew what it was like to hear the landlord knocking on the door.

I knew the fear of poverty. Everyone was your boss and anyone could order you around.

You complied. You ran the errands. You behaved. You drove the cabs. You opened the doors for the rich and then hungered for the tip.

You waited the tables and learned that the cook in the kitchen was your master and king. You fed him his bribes if you knew what was good for you.

You pumped gas and people called you boy.

You made deliveries to the Garment District and you lusted for those models who wouldn't give you a second look because you were in uniform.

You were wearing the uniform of a messenger boy.

You did the telephone soliciting but could get no leads. You mowed the lawns and worked fast in the heat to meet the boss' daily quota.

A flat tire meant your life's savings.

Meantime you took the night courses and learned your craft. You slept with girls who knew people and finally you got your first job.

Then you learned what it was to get fired. There was no problem with your work, but the man had a nephew.

Chapter 22

"I can show you some scenes," I told Adolf.

We were at the Blue Fin on Times Square.

He wasn't listening. He kept eating. Hell, I could do the silent treatment, too.

"Scenes," he finally said.

"Right."

"After all this time, a few scenes?"

"I need more money."

"I expected this. For what?'

"Location scouting."

"Where were you these past two weeks?" he said.

"I thought you knew."

"How should I know?"

"I know you know."

"I need you to tell me," he said.

I said nothing.

"You got a bad habit," he said.

"Don't we all."

"There are no secrets," he said. "Everybody knows everything about everybody. Run, can't hide."

"Ain't that the truth."

"How much?"

I named the figure -- $250,000.

"I already gave you that," he said.

Some people walked by, stopped, ignored him, and asked for my autograph.

"See that?" he said. "You're famous."

"I got spies, too."

"Let's go," he said.

There was no one home. His wife and daughter were out shopping or something.

I showed him some scenes. I started it off with the UN resolution equating Zionism with racism. I did not show what came later, that it was all taken back and made clean. I showed Desmond Tutu declaring himself an anti-Semite, and being satisfied. I showed trains going to Auschwitz but instead of Jews packed inside I showed them as poor bedraggled Palestinians.

Adolf liked that touch.

I showed Yasser Arafat telling American TV that he wanted peace. I did not show what he said in Arabic, that he wanted to drive the Jews into the sea.

I showed Israeli soldiers bulldozing a home and an Arab woman weeping. I did not mention that from this home came a man who had murdered a family of six Israelis, that, in fact, this man had entered the home of these Israelis, murdered the family point blank sleeping in their beds, except for the six-year-old girl who ran from room to room and thought she'd be safe hiding under a bed, but was caught, shot and slain.

I showed Palestinians rushing for food in Ramallah after being starved for days by the Israelis. I did not show that they'd been fasting on their own for a holy day.

I showed Palestinians marching peacefully for peace and did not show the rock throwing and the signs declaring "Death to Israel."

I showed the famous Muhammad al-Dura Incident where the Arab father tried to tuck in his son to protect him against crossfire between Israelis and Palestinians and where immediately the world blamed the Israelis, until it was proven to be false, and even staged. But the incident triggered worldwide outrage even after Israel was exonerated. I did not show that it was all a sham.

"Good," said Adolf.

I showed Jimmy Carter on C-Span, in praise of the Palestinian Arabs and in damnation of the Jews.

"Very good," said Adolf.

I let Jimmy Carter speak of apartheid. I did not show Palestinians sharing shops, jobs, businesses, restaurants, beaches – with Jews. Nor did I show Palestinian Arabs serving as mayors, judges and as members of Israel's parliament, the Knesset. I did not mention that an Arab judge had sent a former president of Israel to jail. That would not fit.

I did not show Palestinian Arabs mocking and molesting a religious Jewish couple in broad daylight in Jerusalem.

I did not show Palestinian mothers proudly adorning their six-year-olds with suicide belts.

I showed multitudes of Palestinians hailing their conquering heroes; cheering the return of 1,200 Palestinian prisoners who'd been held in Israeli jails.

I did not mention that they had been exchanged for one Israeli prisoner, who was dead.

I showed Israelis building illegal outposts on the West Bank, but did not show Arabs building illegal outposts on the West Bank.

I showed Arab and world leaders decrying Israel's lack of initiative for peace.

"This is good," said Adolf.

I did not show Israel's disengagements from Sinai, Hebron and Gaza as concessions for the sake of peace.

I did not show what happened after 10,000 Israelis living in Gaza were moved out in favor of the Palestinians. Everything was burned to the ground. I did not show that, since the takeover, the Palestinians in Gaza, under the rule of Hamas, had showered Israel with 10,000 rockets a month. A million Israelis had to live in bomb shelters and keep running for their lives.

I showed Arab prisoners in Israeli jails on a hunger strike, drawing support and sympathies from around the world.

I did not show that these prisoners had bombed buses, pizza parlors and universities at a cost of 149 Israeli lives.

I showed the king of Jordan demanding more concessions from Israel, saying this was "the last chance for peace."

I did not mention that his father, King Hussein, had killed 10,000 members of the PLO in what is still known as Black September.

"Not bad," said Adolf. "Not bad."

I showed the Incident at the Ramallah Police Station. Two young Israeli IDF reservists lost their way and accidentally wandered into Palestinian territory. They were taken in by police, members of the Palestinian Authority. The kids thought they'd be safe and escorted back home. A mob gathered outside police headquarters demanding blood. The doors were flung open and the mob grabbed the two kids and hacked them to death, and, with the help of the police, mutilated them and lynched them and then tossed their remains out the window. The mob wanted more. One of the attackers approached the window to display his arm dripping blood.

"What's this?"

"Right, I don't know how that got in there," I said.

"Get it out!"

"Sure."

The two victims were Vadim Nurzhitz and Yossi Avrahami.

I did not show the decapitation of Wall Street Journal reporter Daniel Pearl – his throat slit for being Jewish.

I did not show Palestinians dancing in the streets immediately after our Twin Towers went down in Manhattan at a price of 3,000 lives.

I showed Jimmy Carter again listing his grievances against the Jewish State.

I had every intention of burning all this...when the time came.

"You did more than I thought," Adolf said.

"You should be ashamed of yourself for doubting me."

I wasn't totally stupid. I knew the day would come when I'd have to give him something for his money – and now, after what happened, I needed more.

He wrote out a check.

"How soon do you think you'll have it done?"

"Another two to three months, depending."

"On what?"

"Give me a break here," I said.

He said he wanted it presented at film festivals around the globe. He had connections. He could get it to Sundance and Cannes. It was sure to go over big in Europe. France, Sweden, Norway, Denmark, Holland, England, Ireland – they all had appetites for this. They were gluttons for this, especially in those countries where Muslims were coming in and Jews were going out, running for their lives, in droves.

"Can't you quit the gambling?"

"I quit every day."

I got up to leave. I felt filthy.

"Why don't you stay? The ladies should be back any minute."

"I really have to go."

"How are you getting along with Barbara?"

"That's personal."

He reminded me again and again that his daughter Helen had lost a lot of weight.

"She has a crush on you, you know."

"I wouldn't know why."

"Neither would I. But you know women."

"There's no accounting for taste, right?"

"Right."

As for Adolf, Margaret was his second wife, and a trophy. She'd been a model. Now she was Society.

"Do you think," he said, "that this could win an Oscar?"

This wasn't as outrageous as it sounded. Today's Hollywood was likely to side with "the plight of the Palestinians."

"Imagine that," Adolf said. "The Academy Awards."

I left him dreaming.

Chapter 23

I met Jay Garfield for drinks over at P.J. Clarke's.

"You haven't been the same since this started," I told him.

He was a rumpled sort, good looking but rumpled; the classic newspaperman. He could have been in pictures. He ran the *Manhattan Independent*. Now it was months since he'd got himself tangled up with that woman Lyla Crawford, his book review editor; so getting involved with a staffer was bad, and getting involved with a married woman was very bad, and getting involved with a married woman who was married to a man who was part of the same newspaper staff was awfully bad – and to top it all off he had converted to Islam, this husband, and that made it deadly.

"She's got my number," Jay said.

He was thinking of shipping her husband, Phil, off to Israel.

"For what?" I asked.

"To cover the war."

"But Phil Crawford is not one of your foreign correspondents, or so I thought."

"Oh he's been pining for a chance, make him a hero."

Lyla had once caught him being a coward – something like Hemingway's *Short Happy Life of Francis*

Macomber, except here there was no game to make it even.

I asked Jay straight out if he was sending Phil out to get caught in the heat of some battle, to return dead.

Phil gave this some thought.

"Lyla is up to something like that," he said.

"Lyla?"

"The Phil you knew is not the same. You want the stories since he's converted?"

"I can imagine."

"It's worse," Jay said.

"So what are you going to do?"

"There is a legitimate side to this as well. Phil has always wanted to cover the Middle East, and he is a damned good reporter."

"Sounds like an excuse."

"Always comes out the same?"

"It would in court."

"How about you?"

I told him about Barbara, and I told him about Katrina Interlante out in Hollywood.

"So?" he said.

"I couldn't get it done in Hollywood," I confessed.

"What a waste."

"Tell me about it," I said. "But she keeps calling. She says there's unfinished business."

"You have to go."

"I'm still nuts about Barbara."

"After what she did?"

"Call me stupid."

"Can you really forgive?"

"That's what she keeps asking."

"Really."

"She's being quite obvious that she wants to start fresh."

"Figure it never happened."

"I wonder. I wonder if I can ever get it out of my mind."

"Maybe that's what they mean by forgiveness," Jay said.

He laughed when I told him what I had pulled on Adolf.

"Watch out for that guy," Jay said. "He can lay it on you front page." Then he reminded me, "He doesn't use bullets. He uses ink."

Jay Garfield should know.

Chapter 24

Los Angeles is so different from New York! Coming here – from New York – it's like being a stranger in a strange land.

In New York we seek adventure. In LA they seek perfection, and that's mostly about Hollywood and environs that we're talking about.

We're openly brazen. They're deceptively insolent.

There are no potholes in Beverly Hills. There is no graffiti in Santa Barbara.

The ocean was heavenly blue as we walked along Palisades Park.

Katrina wasn't professionally adorned and I liked her better like this, not entirely beautiful but even more desirable.

She was in a serious mood.

"I think you should reconsider Drake's offer," she said, about the feature film he had promised at nothing more than the cost of my integrity.

She'd been reading scripts and there was nothing that she liked and meanwhile her career needed boosting. Her public would soon forget who she was. This wasn't like the old days when movie stars stuck around. Today's shelf life was maybe a year or two and before you knew it you were a has-been. She wanted this part.

"I can't," I said.

"Would you do it for me?"

"Are there no other directors in town?"

"You know they all have their own pets."

This epitome of glamour – her career was in my hands? My friends should see me now. Better yet, my enemies.

For some reason I thought this was all fake, that it wasn't a part in a movie that brought me over. Maybe she just needed someone to talk to, about anything. I knew how it was around here, where in so many lives even or especially among the rich and famous every night was Sunday night.

We went back to her place. She said we didn't have to talk, that she preferred that we just listen to music. She put on Schuman's Rhenish Symphony and she started to cry along about the fourth movement. "He lost his wife, you know – Clara. She fell in love with Brahms. The heartbreak is all over this piece." True, especially that fourth movement.

All art is about sexual longing, I said.

"You mean romantic," she corrected.

"No, sexual."

"Don't you believe in romance?"

I reminded her that I'm from New York. There's no time.

She smiled.

There had been a suicide attempt. Manny Marcus, my agent, told me this over the phone.

Well, they all try this. They give everything a try.

Besides, she was Russian. They bled melodrama.

She missed the melancholy of Russia. There, people knew how to be sad. Here it was all about happiness. Here there was no time, no place, no patience for sadness, and she could think of nothing more boring. She

135

quoted Tolstoy's *all happy families are alike.* She maintained that there had to be a certain shallowness about so much emphasis on perpetual gladness. Life can't always be a sitcom.

"What hurts?" I asked her.

"I don't know," she said. "I really don't know."

"You mean – is that all there is?"

She lit up.

"Something like that," she said.

"We all have such moments."

"I know how ridiculous this is," she said. "You must think I have everything."

"But you don't have love."

"Please don't make fun."

She was drinking wine. I was having vodka and tonic, which she had made mixed with hands of experience. We were on the couch in one of her living rooms – no maids to disturb us – and we both knew the moment would come for another try and, privately, we were both vexed by this. She confessed that her heart was still in Russia. She was as American as the next person – she'd already been here 20 years – but somehow...somehow she did not seem to fit.

"I see everything through the eyes of an immigrant," she said. "Still."

"Exactly what's the issue?" I asked.

"So much plenty in this great land."

"That's a problem?"

"Too much. There's too much of everything. One day, I think, everything will explode and we'll be back to the Stone Age."

I'd thought of that myself. With all our technological gadgets, everything still had to be plugged in – and suppose one day God or whatever pulls the plug?

Hurricane? Earthquake? Meteor?

"Did you talk with Miles Korwin?"

Now the truth was coming out. This was the film critic that had blasted her latest performance and was vindictive to her no matter what she did.

He stalked her.

For her latest role, she had to undergo a screen test.

"I was humiliated."

Stars of her magnitude did not do screen tests.

"I think it's because of Miles," she said. "I *know* it's because of Miles. He's that big. He hates me."

I did talk to him, as I had promised her I would.

"Didn't go well," I said.

"Probably made it worse, huh?"

"He is a son of a bitch."

Now she was afraid to offer herself for any type of role.

"I can't go through with this. Gil, am I finished in the business?"

"Over one bad review?"

"That can do it, you know."

"No it can't," I said.

But yes it can. One bad review can kill. I'd seen it happen. I'd been victimized myself. I had my own Miles Korwins.

They had no talent of their own, so they leeched. They piggybacked. They hounded. They stalked. They win. You lose.

Miles Korwin had certainly won it over Katrina Interlante. He could declare victory. He had succeeded. He had ruined her.

Was it that serious? Yes it was. Was that the suicide? Over one review? Who knows? Who knows another person's breaking point.

"Did I tell you what happened?"

Here comes a story. There is always the story. I learned that from my first day as a newspaper reporter. First the story, then the real story.

"He tried to seduce me."

"In exchange for becoming your friend?"

"That wasn't the language he used, but it was understood."

"Next you'll tell me he tried to rape you."

"He didn't have to," she said.

"Huh?"

"I gave in."

I did not expect that sort of happy ending.

"Say something," she said.

"Well..."

"You don't know what to say. You think less of me."

"Well..."

"From the first time I met you I hoped we would become lovers."

"I wasn't immune."

"You are handsome, and so much more."

"All the girls tell me that," I lied.

She deserved a heap full of credit for being so candid about Miles Korwin. That took guts.

One lousy review – and that was enough to sink her? Make that one lousy reviewer.

"I think I'm in love with you," she said.

"But nothing happened between us," I said.

"Maybe not to you. To me it did. Don't you remember?"

A bunch of us were outside the Hungry Cat restaurant. A scuffle broke out and it was getting dangerous. I saw her leaving but getting caught between flying fists. She tried to run and she tried to duck, but she was trapped. Her chauffeur stayed at the limo when he should have done something. I lifted her up and took her to the safety of her car. Yes, now I remembered.

"No big deal," I said.

She asked if I could love her just today.

"That won't be difficult."

She went upstairs and came down wearing tight jeans and a tight sweater – those curves had no beginning and no end.

"No pressure," she said.

"Right."

"No bedroom. Too much pressure in the bedroom."

"This is true."

I grew tense.

"You're tense," she said.

"How could you tell except that I spilled my drink?"

She laughed.

"We can just play, you know."

"Right. Nothing serious."

"Was it just me the other time?" she asked as she began rubbing my back.

"Sometimes it happens when guys leave town, familiar surroundings."

"Really?"

"You never know. It has a mind of its own."

She liked that and really laughed.

I was beginning to relax.

She stopped, behind me, and I didn't know what she was doing. She came around and faced me with bare breasts.

I massaged them.

"Oooh," she said. "You like my nipples."

I began chewing her nipples.

"Ouch."

"I'm hurting you?"

"No. No. Please."

She slid down, unzipped me – this big movie star, I kept reminding myself – and went to work, expertly. I was hard. But would it last?

For a moment I lost track. I remembered that she had given in to Miles Korwin. Was that cheap, yes, but was it forgivable?

Under the circumstances, who was I to judge?

Her career was at stake – *is* at stake.

Forgiveness seemed to be in the air.

Barbara wanted forgiveness. Yes Barbara. Oh Barbara. "Oh Katrina," I said.

"Are you coming?"

"No. I don't think so."

I watched her at work, moving back and forth, her head bobbing. She did not gaze up at me, as they do, as Barbara did.

Katrina Interlante had her own style. They all had their own style.

I loved the sound of her movements. I reached for her naked breasts and grabbed a handful for play.

She started to undress me and started to undress herself as she led me to her to bedroom. Finally?

Would I perform?

Would I perform as heroically as at that restaurant?

To fail again would be *disaster*.

The thought of that alone could spell defeat.

She sat at the edge of the bed. We both continued our plays. She leaned back and spread her legs. I gripped beneath her knees and pulled her up for traction. I thrust, and got in. "Oh!" she said, and smiled. She watched me as I kept thrusting, but there was still no animation. Her breathing was steady, too steady for me to think that I had reached her where it hurt.

I kept working and waiting for the turn-on moment and I knew it would come when she closed her eyes. She was beginning to turn crimson and that was progress. Our rhythm, of which there had been none at the start – our rhythm began to click, and now we moved as one. She closed her eyes. She began to moan. That's when I took over.

Her climax was wild.

I got off and turned over. I needed a break. I realized that I did not hear her breathing. I turned to her, and she was out, cold. Her arms and legs were slack, no life to them and no life to her eyes, and she wasn't breathing. I shook her to no avail and then I slapped her face gently and then harshly – and she awoke. "What?" I said. "What happened?"

"What you do mean?"

"I thought you were dead."

She said that happened to her sometimes. Actually it only happened to her once before, when she was 17.

"I was travelling," she said.

"What does that explain?"

"Have you ever heard of ecstasy? Well that's where I was, lover."

She hugged me and wept.

"I knew it would be like this," she said.

"Not bad."

I was dying for coffee.

"Coffee?" she laughed. "Are you pregnant or something?"

"I need coffee."

"I'll make you some."

I heard her talking to one of her maids. She came back.

"Coffee and what else?"

"Just coffee."

I was dying for a smoke. No more smoking in this world. I always brought my cigars with me in case I found a sensible corner of civilization.

But I felt good. Damn did I feel good! King of the jungle!

You weren't supposed to ask, but she read my mind.

"Three times," she said. "Couldn't you tell?"

"No."

I wondered if she'd ever climaxed three times for other men – please, let's not get middle class.

She went out and came back with two mugs. Coffee never tasted so good. Life was never this good.

I had conquered Hollywood!

She refused to let me out of bed except to go to the bathroom.

"I'm holding you prisoner," she said.

I tried to get some sleep, but two hours later she woke me. She'd been stroking me and fitted herself in and began the pumping and now we had the rhythm all worked out and she kept me going until it flat-lined, but she was made satisfied. She went back to stroking and I grew in her mouth. She delighted in this, and now she looked up to enjoy my reactions. The jitters were gone and we could have fun.

Two hours later she woke me again, and again we went to work. This went on all night.

Crazy thoughts kept creeping in. Was it like this with everybody? Had it been like this even with Miles Korwin? How could she do Miles Korwin? Well she did and it was done, and worst of all, it didn't work out. His hatred of her – for whatever reason – only increased. How could he respect her after she had traded herself off? Well *she* thought there was going to be a trade. That didn't happen. She had given herself up to save her career and in her business that meant saving your life.

Sex was toy land anyway. Sex was an exchange for favors.

"Will you love me just today?" she said.

"Yes."

"You will?"

"Yes I will."

"Just today. That's all I ask."

"Okay."

"Really?" she said, almost in astonishment.

"Of course."

"More than that would be asking too much."

"Okay."

"I love you," she said.

I always took that to be Hollywood-speak. But was it possible? True love, here, in the land of make-believe?

"I've been in love before," she admitted.

"Of course."

"But never like this."

In the days that followed she only let me out of the house a few times, and these were for trips to the beach.

She did not want me to meet any of her friends.

"I'm keeping you to myself," she said.

She did not want me to get mixed up with her crowd. She was worried something might happen.

"If I fell for you, so can somebody else."

Finally she took me to the back lot at Paramount Pictures. I walked the same balcony that William Holden walked in *Sunset Boulevard*. I met her producer, Danielle Franklin. She extended a big handshake. "I'm always happy to meet a writer from New York," she said. I explained that I did documentaries. "Same thing, no?" Katrina said, "People in Hollywood are always impressed by New York."

"Clash of civilizations," I said.

"I understand that you might be joining us," Danielle said.

"We're in negotiations," I said.

"I'm working on him," Katrina said.

Later I told her that the back lot reminded me of a racetrack's backstretch. I kept looking for the horses and the trainers, finding instead actors and producers. But the graveled roads were about the same, as were the bungalows, not to mention the rush of excitement anticipating what the next day may bring, a winning horse over there, a winning movie over here.

Going with my crowd was okay and we went to Hollywood Park. She had been to the races before, but never with anyone who knew the horses as I did, as I did all too well. I taught her how to play and told her never to bet anything except to win; place and show were for sissies. The thrill was seeing your horse cross the finish line first. There was no sensation like that sensation. "Oh?" she laughed seductively.

She won something like $200. I did well, even after I poured it on in the feature race, when I put down $2,000 to win. Katrina was not surprised that I bet so big. She knew my reputation. She knew that I was a gambler and that I had gambling troubles, all still waiting when I got back home. I had told her nearly everything, and she made no judgments and gave no lectures. I was proud of her. She was a winner.

Back in Santa Monica I asked Katrina to explain why this fascination with New Yorkers.

"We think New York is the real deal. Around here we're just pretending. We are the lightweights. New York has the heavyweights."

We made love for several more days.

She did not want me to leave.

"Love me for one more day."

She was a needy child.

I was falling in love with her.

Barbara (and a few hundred others) had been phoning, but I hadn't picked up, but this time I did.

"It's your mom," she said.

Chapter 25

I took the next plane back and arrived at Kessinger's Communal Living Estates the next morning. Barbara was there, waiting for me. She intercepted me before I marched into my parents' bungalow; Dad being overly upset. Mom, it turned out, had not been diligent in her work. Residents who failed to perform were assumed to be unwell and taken to the hospital – and there was a hospital on the grounds. Once in, few got out.

We knew about this from the start, that Kessinger's expected each resident to do a job. Charles Kessinger had explained it during the days of indoctrination, saying that the process was important to keep seniors fit, nimble and able. Made sense, made perfect sense. Each resident worked an hour a day and had a quota to fulfill, and each "section" had different duties along different assembly lines. Mom and Dad had been assigned to the lamp-designing quarter. The work was not difficult, was even fun and relaxing and was meant to give the residents a sense of purpose plus the satisfaction of achievement. Made sense.

"We are not like nursing homes," Charles Kessinger had announced, "where seniors are warehoused to waste away."

Yes, Kessinger's was different, but if a particular resident showed signs of slacking, he or she was placed under observation, and if still among the un-quick, was moved to the Recuperating Room from which, according to Dad, they were starved to death. I had seen the Recuperating Room and it was a terrible sight to behold; people there were truly emaciated – but under the constant care of doctors and nurses. But who were these doctors and these nurses?

Mom's job had been to apply lacquer to the finish of those lamps, but, hands stiffened from arthritis, she could not even curl her palm around the brush and so she had fallen behind on the assembly line. She had hoped no one would notice, but supervisors were always on hand, and strangely, her neighboring workers informed on her. They pointed her out to the supervisors.

Mom had tried to catch up and that led to fumbling, until she finally dropped one of the lamps.

"Residents are on their own," Kessinger liked to say. "We do not encourage helping out as that makes people dependent."

Yes, residents, the elderly, seniors, that is, had to learn vitality; they had to take baby steps to get up and stand again – without assistance.

Made sense.

But the tattling – that was disturbing. But Charles Kessinger had a reason for that, too: "They have to be reminded what it's like in the real world."

In the real world there wasn't much time for mercy, compassion or kindheartedness.

"Our people have to learn that," Charles Kessinger said, "unless they forgot."

That too made sense. Look around. Read the headlines.

Charles Kessinger was quick to point out that compassion was rare around the world and that even in the

United States there wasn't much neighborliness, if only because there were no more neighborhoods, nothing like there were in the past, when people of a kind lived together and stuck together, whereas these days even families lived apart, children from children, fathers from sons, mothers from daughters, and in many cases wives from husbands and husbands from wives – all living apart.

"We want our people re-trained, re-educated, re-conditioned, and ready to go," Charles Kessinger liked to say.

Road rage was everywhere and residents had to be taught that a green light does not necessarily mean go and red does not always mean stop.

Life was yellow – take your chances. Do not reach out for a helping hand.

"I'm afraid he's going for another stroke," Barbara said.

Dad had already had two, only they had been diagnosed as mini-strokes, but still serious, too serious, far too serious to bring him back home, and even far too serious to enroll him, and Mom, anywhere else. They were all the same, and here there were doctors and nurses and a constant watch. It did not get any better than this. This was the paradise for seniors.

"They're starving your mother, you know," Dad said.

"We'll get her out," I said.

"Better be quick before they finish her off."

He was weeping.

"How long ago did this happen?"

"Two days ago," Barbara said.

"Why didn't you answer her when she kept calling?" Dad asked.

"I was away."

Dad let that sit, but Barbara gave me a look.

"No," I whispered. "I wasn't out gambling."

Dad knew about my gambling, but he never troubled me on that vice. He was a great man and a great writer. He understood weakness.

He wrote about weakness and the traps we fall into in the name of temptation. His biggest bestseller was on that topic.

So he never touched me on my defects and he loved me and I loved him. He never lifted a hand against me when I was growing and still growing up.

Dad without Mom was unimaginable.

"We'll take care of it," I assured him.

He shot me a special glance, and soon I remembered that he had used that same line in *Heaven's Guest* to indicate futility. Over the years he never read his books after they'd been published as that would be a particular act of vanity, and besides, he would already be upon his next work. But lately (Mom had told me) he did turn a few pages to prove to himself that he had once been Joseph Gilels and not some anonymous old-timer decaying in a nursing home.

He had seen all my documentaries and was proud enough to self-deprecatingly tell the world that he was the father of Gil Gilels.

"Is there anyone to talk to in this place?" he asked.

"We're going to find out."

"Go directly to the top," he said. "Always go directly to the top."

"I know that, Dad."

"Nothing moves until the man at the top says so."

"That's true," said Barbara.

"I know this from experience," said Dad.

He tried to collect himself and to believe in our assurances. He was afraid to be taken for an angry old man. He was not an angry old man, but he was an old man. He was so sure that there was still life ahead – even here he was somehow sure of that, as long as Mom was at his side. There were still books that needed to be written. He was still at his typewriter, but not since Mom had been taken. He even chanced writing his Ninth novel, never mind the Beethoven curse.

"You have to bring her back," he said.

"We will," Barbara said.

"In any condition," he said.

"Yes," I said.

"Who knows what they did to her," he said.

"They have doctors."

"No, they are killers."

"The State checks them out, Dad."

"They hide the bodies," he said. "You've seen the so-called recuperation room."

Yes, we had seen it, and without a doubt it was a place nobody wanted to be near. They were like zombies, those who were taken to "recuperate." Charles Kessinger had explained that some of the residents refused to eat, intentionally starving themselves. This was a serious problem faced by the doctors and the nurses who kept trying to maintain strict dietary conditions.

"No," said Dad. "Food is being denied them. The purpose is to get them out, get them buried – move product."

Charles Kessinger had told us that force-feeding was against federal law.

"Has it occurred to anyone that this place and places like this are all part of a big federal program?" asked Dad.

"To do what?" I asked.

"To get rid of people after a certain age!"

"That's a movie, Dad."

"*This* is no movie, this place."

"All right..."

"These doctors, so-called, they are all so young. Where were they trained? Notice again how professionally discourteous they are, all of them."

"Some of them are okay."

"Those plastic smiles? Now that's a movie."

He had been walking around with his cane, and now sat down at his desk, in front of his typewriter, certainly not to write, but this was his place of comfort and security. Around home, during any disturbance or disruption, as when the heater went bust and flooded the floors, Dad immediately took action, right at his desk, and it was the same the few times he got into a spat with Mom; he'd go right to his desk, his seat of power, though Mom usually won anyway.

Sometimes he'd start writing and couldn't stop and Mom would never disturb him, even if dinner started getting cold. She'd just start over again when he was ready, and sometimes he wrote deep into the night, and we knew that at such hours he was at his best, when the words wouldn't stop. There were stretches like that, he told us, later, when we were older, when the words seemed to drop from heaven, messages that he, the writer, couldn't figure out, so that it was like taking dictation.

When the inspiration took hold of him like that – that's when he got absentminded and forgot where he left his car keys, even his car, and even his kids, as once happened in the mall; he'd be so lost in thought. Even to stop off for bread and milk, Mom would write it out for him because she knew the book and only the book was on his mind. I missed those days. Sometimes they were quite funny and once in a while quite hilarious.

We had a good home – and now this!

Barbara and I went over to the recuperation room. She wasn't so ill as to be bedridden, so they had her seated in some sort of living room with old people sitting and groaning. She appeared to be okay! Her hair had not yet turned to complete gray and her face still had fine coloring, and not much of that was faded, even now, and at our approach she got up, hugged us and kissed us.

"How's your father?" she asked.

"He's doing okay," we both lied.

"You're lying, of course."

"Why are you here, Mom?"

She'd just fallen asleep at the switch, she said, and the supervisors at the shop were worried about her.

"Dad thinks there's a conspiracy," I said.

"I don't think so."

"They put you here awfully fast," Barbara said.

"I was surprised," Mom admitted. "Come clean about your father. Don't worry about me. "

"Whom do we talk to around here?"

I meant in terms of a supervisor. The residents surrounding my mom were in a terrible state, and truly emaciated.

"The office is over there," Mom said.

"We'll be right back."

Barbara and I went over to the office where two female clerks were busy at their computers and did not look up at our approach. Barbara and I waited for some attention and the younger one finally asked, "What can I do for you?" We explained the situation. "We can't let her go until the director signs her out."

"Where can we find the director?" asked Barbara.

The older clerk spoke up. "Dr. Donald is on rounds."

"When will he be *off* rounds?" asked Barbara.

The both of them asked the both of us to speak quietly. The patients must not be disturbed.

"Depends," said the younger one.

"On what?" I asked.

"Depends how long it takes," said the older one.

"We don't believe Mrs. Gilels belongs in here," said Barbara.

"That's for Dr. Donald to decide," said the younger one.

"How about the State Police?" I said.

They both said, "I beg your pardon?"

I spoke softly and quietly and carefully, saying, "If my mother is not out of here within half an hour I am going to the police."

The younger one asked the older one if Charles Kessinger was on the grounds.

"Tell him," I said, "that I will have the police check on him, too."

At the door, I said, "Half an hour."

Barbara and I went back, but Mom was not there, standing or sitting. One of the residents said, "She went up to the room."

I went back to the two clerks.

"She must have gone up to the room."

"Is there a phone?"

She phoned. Mom answered. I asked her what she was doing.

"Packing my things."

"Good girl," I said. "You'll be out of here in half an hour."

Dad did not like scenes. He did not like hello, he did not like goodbye, he did not like birthdays and he did not like holidays, so when we brought her back, he said, "Shopping again?" Mom knew what to expect, so she waited a while before they kissed; married all these years and they kissed like a couple on their first date.

I'd have to get them out before it was too late.

Chapter 26

I took Barbara for coffee. She had her radio show to do in a couple of hours and I did not want to detain her, but she seemed in no hurry.

"I missed you," she said.

I was still wearing Katrina.

"I was out of town," I said.

She stirred her coffee. I remembered that she didn't like Starbuck's coffee. Neither did I.

"I know you were in Hollywood. Is this about that movie for Drake Goldsmith?"

I wasn't sure if she was on to me about Katrina, or if she really didn't know. Despite her sophistication, she could be quite naïve.

"Something like that," I said.

She kept stirring her coffee.

"I hear that Katrina Interlante is interested," she said.

"So are quite a few others."

"But she wants it really bad."

The part, or me? I couldn't make her out and I wasn't about to reveal what really happened, though why should I care?

Really, why should I care?

The wound was still open.

"Did you spend time with her?"

"Who?"

"Gil, please."

"I saw her a few times."

Her face turned red, and I thought she was about to cry.

"Do you care for her?"

"Barbara, what about you? Aren't you seeing somebody?"

"Nobody. I'm seeing nobody."

"Too busy, huh?"

"I'm just not interested."

No, I was not about to bring up James Headley.

"What about James Headley?"

"That's cruel," she said.

"You bet," I said.

Normally she'd bolt. But she stayed.

"Do we have to do this every time? Don't you say life goes on?"

Indeed I do. But what did I have going on here? I was still intoxicated with Katrina but somehow, for some reason, still in love with Barbara, and there was something quite touching about Barbara all of a sudden. The games were over, for her. The role-playing was done. She had ditched the sophistication and had left the cynicism up to me.

"Life goes on," I said.

"That's more like it," she said, brightening. "That's better."

"Shouldn't you be going?"

"I've got time."

"Usually you rush with four hours to go."

"Did something happen between you and Katrina?"

I shook my head.

"I'd like to know."

"What's the difference?" I said.

"I need to know."

"You're jealous?"

"It's more than that," she said.

"Oh?"

"I need to know if it's worth pursuing you."

"Actually I have to run," I said.

She got up and moved quickly for the door. I got up slowly. She slowed down waiting for me to catch up. But I headed straight for the off-track betting.

Chapter 27

For about the first time in my career as a gambler – and really, it was a career -- I was worried. Adolf's money wasn't holding. One morning I woke up to realize that I was near broke again – and still owed. I was behind on the rent and I was behind on big men who wanted their money *now*. This affected my eating and my sleeping and I was starting to lose weight. The tooth problems were back and I suffered bouts of migraines. Stress, people told me.

I knew this wasn't any good on the day that blizzard hit. Nothing was moving. Everything was shut down. Schools were closed and even government workers were told not to report. The wind kept howling and the snow kept piling up. There were no cars on the roads. We were told to stay put until it passed, making it sound like a plague.

But I had places to go. I had picked out the entire card at Aqueduct. I was convinced that I had the winner in every race. Why should I let stupid weather stop me? The off-track betting parlors were closed; this I knew. But perhaps Aqueduct was open. There was no chance of that, except a fraction of one percent, enough to get me dressed and ready to go. I phoned the track and there was no answer except for the automation. This was not so unusual, being unable to get through. I kept phoning on the chance that someone would pick up, but nothing came back.

No, I was hoping no one would answer because if someone did pick up, I'd most likely hear that the track was closed – and they wouldn't be nice about it, either, whoever answered. "Are you crazy?" they'd say.

No, I just want to know if you're open.

"You must be nuts, Mister."

Will you be opening late?

"Are you kidding? Have you looked outside?"

Doesn't look so bad.

"What's your name?"

Why?

"Someone ought to report you."

I'm only asking if you're just postponing instead of cancelling.

"You need help, Mister."

Hey, that's rude.

"You need intervention."

I can take care of myself.

"You're not a horseplayer."

Yes I am.

"You're a compulsive gambler. You are sick."

Now that is terribly rude.

"Fuck you, Mister. How's that for rude?"

I thought I heard a report on TV that all racetracks were shut down as well as everything else but turned it off before I could hear the full report. Maybe they were closed but were opening late. There you go! That had happened a few times before. Or maybe they were starting early and would close up later when the jockeys refused to ride because of the weather conditions. This had also happened – and quite a few times in the past. That would be good enough for me because the sure things I had were on the early races. Yes, that would be good enough. Can't bet early and often? Well just bet early.

I could have checked Aqueduct's website, but I didn't want to know. I only wanted to know that there was a chance.

I could not have done all that handicapping for nothing, and another chance as good as this one, where all my choices seemed so certain, might never come round again. If it's your day, it's your day, and it would be criminal to put it to waste. There were days like that, when you could not lose, but you had better show up. This would be a nasty trick to have all my horses win while I dithered because of some snow.

I got dressed, doubled up on all my clothes, and started for the elevator to take me down to the garage on the corner where my car was parked. Ordinarily I would have taken the Racetrack Special, but no trains or buses were running. The elevator started going down and then stopped between floors. I felt it rattling and I felt and heard the vibrations coming from the howling wind. I pressed buttons going up or down but nothing happened and then I pressed the red button and the bell rang even as I knew there'd be no response because these bells often rang and nobody in the building ever paid much attention.

I tried my cell phone but got no reception. I wasn't worried about being stuck, only about missing the first race. I began pounding on the doors, and then I tried to pry them open, which I did, only to have them shut back again. There was a stool here, still from the days when they were manually operated – this was an old, actually historic apartment complex – and got myself up to the roof of the elevator, and it took some doing but I climbed up into a shaft, climbed further hanging onto the ropes, found a set of doors, and using all my strength, got them to open, and found myself plunged onto the 16ᵗʰ floor.

I ran down the steps. Outside I found it to be worse than what it looked like from the window. The blizzard had come like an invasion. It was nearly impossible to walk against the wind and against the quickly gathering snow. But I walked. Roberto wasn't there at his station in the parking lot, and the arm was up to prevent cars going in or coming out. I found my car and crashed the arm. I would pay for the damage later.

I started driving. The car refused to move. I kept accelerating until I got some movement and started making some headway, even as the wind and snow kept slashing my windshield. I could barely see. The street signs were covered and the roads and sidewalks were one mountain of snow. But I knew the route automatically, having made this trip so often.

Somehow I got myself onto the Parkway – the only vehicle anywhere in sight – and began to visualize myself at the track, placing my bets, and watching my horses run. I turned on the radio and it was all about the weather and the dangers of the road. Fortunately, the radio said, there were few accidents, so far, because people were smart enough to stay indoors.

"Everything is closed, shut down," said the announcer.

But he did not mention Aqueduct specifically. I knew the exit to the track and though I could not see clearly and though all exit signs were covered in snow, I knew that I was getting close. I could do no more than about 20 miles an hour, and even then my car kept swerving, but I should be no more than two miles from my destination. I had been driving for two hours and 20 minutes when ordinarily it took me 40 minutes on a good day. But I kept driving with no end in sight.

I wondered if I had turned onto the wrong Parkway. There was nothing but highway straight ahead. There was no place to turn off. All the exits were blocked and all the road signs were indecipherable. My GPS wasn't working because it never worked and it was my fault that I never took it back to the dealer. I was afraid to stop. The car might get stuck and not move again. The car kept skidding but I managed to get some mileage, only I did not know where I was headed.

Now I started to get exhausted. I had to keep hard on the steering wheel or else I'd be off the road and into a ditch. I thought I saw mountains up ahead, but it was blurry for the slashing wind and snow. I had turned the radio off but now I turned it back on and it said that all major highways were closed. So where was I? I was hungry and thirsty and began to drift.

I had fallen asleep for about 10 seconds but it was enough to get me sliding into a ditch, but I pulled back just in time. I drove on. Finally, some life. I saw a man walking across the divider. I could barely make him out, but it appeared to be someone trudging against the tides of snow. "Hey," I yelled. He kept walking. "Hey, can you hear me?"

I'd have to stop, but I knew that would get me in big trouble. Where was he going? Where could he be going? Then he disappeared.

I checked my cell phone and decided to make some calls. There were moments when it felt like I was on some other planet. I was certainly far from any civilization that I knew. First I tried Jay Garfield but there was no answer, likewise Barbara and Jake Delahouse and Mike Stanton and Stu Mayer and Johnny Castle, friends from my filmmaking business until it dawned on me that I really had no friends, no real friends, none except for Jay and Barbara, and they weren't answering.

No wonder. The radio said that this massive storm had cut out even cell phone service. This had been my nightmare.

God had pulled the plug.

Really? I had no friends? After a lifetime of high school, college, work, play – no friends? No one to count on? Wait. Johnny Castle was indeed a friend and true.

There were others, but I could not think of them at the moment.

After a career in the film business, and there was nobody around? They were there for my awards. Yes, they were there for my awards. Maybe it was my fault. I never went to their parties. I should have gone to their weddings, their birthdays, their funerals, but I never went. I did go to the races, or, I was busy on a film project, or, I had inherited my disdain for festivities of any kind from my father. They could never count on me, so how could I count on them?

But to have no friends, this was an awakening. There certainly was no one from the racetracks or from my other gambling activities that I could call a friend. No, they were gambling buddies and nothing more and when that day's races were over that day's friendship was over. I did *know* many people and many people knew me, but that never counted for much.

This was no time for guilt or feeling sorry for myself. I avoided happy occasions for fear of the evil eye and for the same reason never whooped it up after a win. No, that was not my style and I really did believe that someone up there was watching and taking account and then deciding how to divvy out your rewards against your punishments. Gambling taught me that lesson.

Never show your hand.

No, never mind the guilt. Other people also made mistakes. Other people were also at fault. You can't take all the blame. Who was I fooling as I kept toying with Adolf, and even with Barbara, and even with Katrina? Who was I fooling when I thought one day there'd be That Day at the track? The odds were never in your favor, certainly not at the tables, and not even at the track.

Yes, but some people did win. Some people.

Of all the girls I had dated, how many would remember me, remember me fondly? Oh please! Not that, please.

How much damage had I done and how much damage had been done unto me?

Now we're getting religious all of a sudden? If we believe in God so fervently, why do we pray only at the track and never at church or synagogue? Dad had told me that God awaits each member of the congregation for services, expects them by name. Instead, He expects me at Aqueduct. My house of worship, Aqueduct. My place of prayer, the casinos. That's where You will find me and that is where You can count on me, O Lord. Too late to get religious. I let Him down and now He is getting even...and I never got that part, that part I never got, the punishments that await us if we don't behave according to the wishes of our ministers, priests or rabbis, who are not themselves so holy.

But is that God's entire business – getting even, taking revenge, meting out punishment? What about His 13 Attributes of Divine Mercy?

When does that click in?

Or is everything sinful?

Like Kafka said, first we convict and pronounce sentence and then we hear testimony.

Or like Torquemada said, show me 20 words written by any man and I will find a reason to hang him.

Hah! Johnny Castle had tried to talk me into doing porn. He did it himself just to keep the pot boiling between legit jobs, although porn was plenty legit, big business, and practically everybody was doing it left and right. "Easy money," he said, "and you can do it at home." I laughed. Barbara didn't. She was game, but only for ourselves. No, the trick was to do it for the money, for the 200 million Americans who watched porn more than they watched *Citizen Kane* or *Casablanca*. There was no business like the porn business.

We tried it a few times, and it was a turn on, knowing the camera was going.

There was one split second when, so happy with her appearance and her performance, that she was ready to volunteer to go public. "All women are exhibitionists," she said. She certainly had performed well, and of all the girls, of all the women, of all the movie stars, there was still only Barbara. Then she did what she did.

Did she do it to spite me and my gambling? We had a good marriage, we had a wonderful marriage, so exactly what was so wonderful about the other guy, James Headley, who was not so wonderful anymore, apparently. She saw the light. I saw him once and tried to figure out what was so attractive about him in the first place. He had bushy eyebrows, beady eyes, a week's growth that passed for a beard, altogether this was no Prince Charming, no George Clooney. Obviously he didn't gamble and obviously he could quote Shakespeare. There was no figuring this out – never was when it came to the dangers of attraction.

So now she had enough of him and she wanted to make amends.

Hail started coming down and now it was treacherous and up ahead there was nothing but more road, more hail, more snow, more wind, more road. It occurred to me, gradually, that this could be my end. For some reason, the thought did not trouble me as much as it should have. After all, I had not done too badly. I had left something behind; I'd say about five, no, six, classic documentaries, and they were still being shown. Then before that there had been the paper journalism, one of which was up for a Pulitzer.

Did I ever make a difference? Yes, my documentary on FGM – *The Sorrow of Female Genital Mutilation* – was still being used by the United Nations to halt that practice.

So the work never dies, and what were you? You were flesh and blood.

I would never get to be the Second Coming of David Lean. It was from Lean that I got the inspiration to go into Film. *Lawrence of Arabia* did it for me, the crisp dialogue, the breathtaking camerawork, namely that cut from the blown out match to the sun-blinding desert; this was my Michelangelo, my Beethoven. In every film I did, I kept David Lean in the back of my mind, imagining him directing me from scene to scene. He had no use for actors. He seldom spoke to them as people. This too I understood, but not to that degree. He was fanatical about getting it right, ruthless to the spirit of the art. Between takes Jack Hawkins had begun horsing around; Lean was furious about the disrespect. I studied *Lawrence*. Each time I learned something new.

Would I get the chance to learn more?

Michael Wilson wrote the first screenplay but Lean was not happy with it because it was too political and unfocused. It had everything about the Revolt in the Desert and that was the problem; it had everything but a center, a hero. Lean hired Robert Bolt. He instructed Bolt to zero in on one man, Lawrence, and have the universe revolve around Lawrence, and let the rest fall into place – and it sure did.

From this I learned to keep my documentaries pointed to a hero, man or woman. There was always one person who made the difference. I was never taken by ensemble casting, even before I was introduced to Lean. Too much going on. As soon as you got interested in one character, another character showed up – and a movie is about two (or one) movie stars.

So I thought of David Lean to keep my mind from *drifting*.

Maybe I should just stop the car. It wasn't going any place anyway. So maybe I should just stop the car and forget everything and let whatever happens happen. This thought gave me comfort. Imagine, no more debts – and that alone gave me comfort. No more debts, no more threats, no more schedules to keep, no more people to please, no more enemies to make; not such a bad deal after all. A few people would miss me.

I was sure to make the news. I had a name. I could have been a contender, and I was. I didn't do all that bad. I could just wait here in the car and let it come, or, if I was really serious, I could get out, walk about half a mile, and freeze to death. No, that would be suicide, and a sin. If I just sat here it wouldn't be my fault. That would make it a pure accident.

But then, on second thought, I would miss the Kentucky Derby!

I'd miss the sight of a naked woman. Better yet, a woman getting undressed, slowly, for you, just for you, and giving you that look.

Barbara had finally learned to masturbate (as if she didn't know it all along) and calling me into the bathroom to catch her unawares, she'd tarry in there to make sure I heard her heavy breathing, and that was quite sensational. But that was nothing to be thinking about at this time. Someone was watching and taking notes and questions would be asked, and besides, like the man said, sex is nothing. Temptation is everything.

Well, that depends.

What did she want? What does woman want? King David had sinned a great sin. He had coveted a married woman, Bathsheba. He sent her husband out to the heat of the heaviest fighting so that he would never return, and so it was. King David then married Bathsheba and for that sin, their first son immediately died. David prayed for forgiveness. He wrote Psalms for forgiveness. David was the father of forgiveness. So next came Solomon, later to be King Solomon, the wisest ruler of them all – and all from the coupling of David and Bathsheba.

Therefore sin, retribution, atonement, forgiveness, the four true elements of an examined life.

What was up there besides nothing? Were those really mountains or a mirage? The car began spinning out of control and with great effort I set it right and kept on going. Through it all the sun had been shining, even blazing, and now it was dusk, and for sure all the races were over, as if I didn't know, all along, that the track was closed. I knew it all along but I still had to go. Such was the urge. Such was the disease? Barbara would again call it the Anatomy of a Compulsive Gambler.

She would probably do a radio show on the topic.

Love me just one more day, Katrina had said. Just one more day. Oh how they needed to be loved!

But such was this craving of mine. I had to go. I had the horses picked out and they could not do this to me.

I certainly was not on the road to Aqueduct, not after all this time. Now banks of snow started coming my way and my car began to lurch, fighting for traction. I steered this way and that but kept slipping and sliding yet somehow kept moving forward, up, up, it seemed, toward those mountain ranges. There were no mountains on the Parkway.

My phone buzzed and it was Barbara, and it got to be like this...HELLO?...HELLO?...HELLO?

But other than that, no reception, and then Jay phoned, and it was the same thing all over again.

Even over dead phones I said that I should be on the Belt Parkway. That is what I told 911 and was told it was impossible to get me out.

What was I doing there anyway?

Now the car refused to move and it even quit idling. The engine was out. I kept trying to start it up again but it was no use. The heater conked out. Now it was freezing. I hadn't brought enough clothes, or food, or even my medicines. I got out and like an idiot checked under the hood, as if I knew what I was doing. I knew nothing mechanical, except for the cameras.

I couldn't even fix a flat tire. My gawd – how pampered and spoiled we are in the big cities, especially Manhattan. Everything is there for us just for the asking.

I started to tinker under the hood, tightening bolts and whatever else might be loose, but my fingers soon froze up and I ran back inside the car, and now it was dark, and here was the moon and stars, and still the wind howling, and still the snow and hail lashing. I had a hundred or so numbers programmed in my iPhone and I tried them all, but nothing came back.

I could not even tell people where I was if they asked me, though I should be, yes should be on Belt Parkway, but nothing here resembled Belt Parkway.

I got angry. I thought of all the spitefulness, double-dealing and double-crossing I'd endured. Jake Emery had a decision to make and he chose the other guy, the other director, and Jake had been Best Man at my wedding and, at his urging, we had made plans to go partners. We were going to astonish the world with our films, first documentaries and then features, big feature films, and we even had some backing lined up, and then he made the decision to cut me under.

He never phoned to explain, certainly never to apologize. No, he found a better deal. He simply found a better deal.

The deal fell apart.

If I got out of all this, would I return to forgive or to get even? No, I would get even, and Jake was not the only one. There were scores of them.

I started pounding the steering wheel and heard myself yelling and I got furious gazing up ahead at all that absolute nothingness. There was nothing but a terrible whiteness that covered the earth, around and around, top to bottom, and there were no sounds except for the punishing wind and the slashing hail. I tried again and *eureka*[!] the car started.

I pushed on ahead, trusting that somewhere up ahead there would be a form of life. There must be.

I turned the radio back on, but voices annoyed me, music annoyed me. I listened for the news, and it was mostly the weather, how awful it was, and that it could take weeks to recover. The cost could run into the billions. Limbs and even trees had crashed into electrical systems and cars and even homes had been crushed. The governor was already demanding disaster relief.

This was the worst storm of the century.

The entire state was shut down and in Washington, D.C., the federal government was shut down, here in the most powerful nation on earth, yes, here, even here all that can happen, all was helpless and futile when God pulled the plug. Wires and batteries held us together and we thought that was enough, but to Nature that was lipstick and chewing gum.

One snowfall – and we were out of luck and out of business.

One report had it that members of Congress and the Supreme Court had fled their buildings and were scattered and on the run throughout the streets of the capital trying to find shelter. These, along with the President, the President of the United States, were the most powerful men and women on earth – and all of it was nothing but vanity. One snowfall and they were licked. What advice, what help could they give when they themselves were destitute?

God gazed down upon the earth and said, so you have built for yourselves another tower, as in Babel – well, now see how you run.

There was more talk on the radio now about evacuations wherever traffic would allow and where the storm had not yet come rushing in. The highways were congested with panicked citizens fleeing their homes. Police spokesmen were saying they'd never seen anything like this. "Armageddon" people kept saying. Airports were closed in five states. Passengers were stranded.

"If you were fool enough to hit the road, forget about getting help," said the announcer.

He only lacked my name.

"Firefighters, police and the National Guard are doing the best they can, but they have their hands full."

"You have to be insane to take the chance," said his partner.

"But there's always a few knuckleheads out there."

"Yes, and they put responders at risk."

"Right, that's the height of selfishness."

I turned off the radio and stopped the car. What was the use driving? Best bet would be to sit it out, and wait till it blew over.

I turned the radio back on.

The weather person was speaking: "There's another storm looming right behind this one."

One wasn't enough.

A collision of weather patterns, said the weather person.

"The perfect storm?" asked the announcer.

"Something like it," she said.

What was that up ahead – a tornado? Or was that just snow spinning and twirling? No, it was a tornado. The radio had said to watch out for them. Tornados had been spotted throughout the eastern part of the state. I watched this incredible Biblical sight, lightning whirling in a bottle; no, the finger of God. I immediately thought of the movie *Out of Africa*: "God is coming."

I drove on. I decided against waiting it out. There had to be an end to this somewhere. I thought I saw a turn-off. I thought I saw an exit sign and then an exit. I gunned the engine but that made it worse, so I coasted. I got to where there was indeed an exit and the semblance of a clearing right at the ramp. I angled right, and pushed into it but the snow was packed too tight and each time it cleared the wind packed in more snow, like setting a trap.

Each time I made for it, more snow came piling on. I got out of the car. I started kicking the mounds of snow to create a clearing, and when I thought I had a clearing I ran back to the car and gunned for it again – and again the clearing packed up. Man against Nature? Not a good bet.

This was not going to work, but here I was going to stay. Here I would wait it out. But how long would it take?

By this time I was nearly too exhausted to care. I must have fallen asleep.

Chapter 28

The item made it to the papers and spread along the Internet. A helicopter had spotted me and four hours later I was being treated for exhaustion and frostbite, and where else but the Aqueduct Medical Center; so I'd made it to Aqueduct after all, one way or another. The talk, even on Page Six, which was the one place you did not want to embarrass yourself, was that I had meant to kill myself – why else would a sane man go out in that weather?

Or, as Adolf Gruberman had it planted and specified in his *Manhattan Voice*, I was despondent over a failure to produce a promised documentary...

Plus suicide over gambling losses.

Jay Garfield's *Manhattan Independent* was equally full of spice.

"I couldn't help it," Jay said over drinks at McSorley's.

He had Lyla with him, Lyla Crawford, his book page editor who should not be seen with him.

"No problem," I said.

His gossip columnist, a terrible woman named Francis Hamm, had no love for me or for Jay, her boss.

Jay ran the paper, a paper that was so split politically that more often than not he was odd man out.

He had fought against naming Jerusalem "occupied territory" at the dateline and had lost. Lyla's husband, byline Phil Crawford, was out there covering the war. His stories were slanted for the Palestinian Arabs and against the Israelis and as often as Jay tried to catch it in time, the obvious slanders, he was too late or overruled. His boss, the publisher Ben Hawkins, was the famous Brit who usually took Jay's side, but he too kept getting overruled by his oil interests and by the sheik that had, somehow, bought in for seven percent of the company.

"Aren't you two kids in trouble?" I said.

The rumor had it that Jay and Lyla had conspired to send her husband out there in the heat of the fiercest battle to get himself killed.

Shades of David, Uriah and Bathsheba.

She was a stunner, Lyla. I could see the problem. He'd been keeping her under wraps, but now, apparently, he wanted to show her off, or maybe he just didn't care anymore. He was being crucified regardless, whether the rumors were true or not. I knew that there'd been problems in her marriage with Phil even before he converted to Islam. After he converted, Phil demanded that she cover up, as their women must, and that she bow to his imam.

There was also some violence.

Lyla promoted fresh voices in her book pages at the *Manhattan Independent* and she'd been admired around town until all that happened.

These were two ruined people sitting in front of me and I wasn't sure whether they knew it or not. They were now prey to all sorts of gossip mongering and it wasn't wearing well on them, despite Lyla's natural beauty. Jay tried to keep it upbeat, but he was at the approach of utter defeat – and no man's career had ever been more promising than Jay's over at the newspaper.

Lyla was forthright enough to admit that these were not the best of times. Friends were departing and enemies were piling in and piling on. Writers that she'd babied and nurtured and nourished were now snubbing her and pasturing elsewhere. First to quit on her were her university colleagues, followed by speeches and lectures she was scheduled to give, abruptly cancelled.

"I guess we have it coming," she said.

"Stop it," Jay said.

Jay was a brawler, but he was about to get fired, along with Lyla.

"It is odd," said Lyla, "that we always seem to meet the right person one person too late."

They'd been after Jay's hide even before the love triangle, for his smoking, his gambling, his love of boxing, mainly his political incorrectness. He wanted it said fairly and squarely up front, both sides of the story, any story, with no interference from personal biases and prejudices and to desist from the kind of journalism that was being practiced these days.

"Were you really on your way to Aqueduct?" Jay said, laughing.

"I refuse to believe this," said Lyla.

"Oh I believe it," said Jay. "I know how it is."

"You guys and your horses," said Lyla.

"Gil has a system," said Jay. "Tell."

"Never mind," I said.

"Oh come on," said Lyla.

"Gil has certain numbers he bets all the time."

"Not all the time."

"Numerology?" asked Lyla.

"It's more than that," I said.

"I happen to believe in numerology," said Lyla. "Perhaps I'm not totally convinced that specific numbers preordain our lives, but I do think there is something else out there that, to a degree, determines our actions and our fate. Free will, I think, is only part of the puzzle that makes us tick."

Jay turned to her in seriousness.

"So this pickle we're in has already been written?"

"Nothing is written," I said, and Jay gave me a high-five knowing that to be a quote from *Lawrence of Arabia*.

"We won't know till it's over," said Lyla.

She was putting up a brave face, but I knew she was hurting. Her husband was out there in a hot combat zone and if he got to meet his end, they were doomed as well. What could they have been thinking, and whose plan had this been in the first place? My guess was Lyla, although Jay was no pushover. So is this love, or is this where temptation leads? Wasn't I in the same boat?

Lyla had an appointment at a bookstore. A writer she knew was giving a talk. Jay and I went to the races to place a few bets.

"Newsroom gossip tells me that you're in deep shit with Gruberman," Jay said.

"That's no gossip, Jay."

"I'm told he's prepared to start printing stories about you, and you know what that can do."

"Yes."

"Are you listening?"

"Word for word."

"That motherfucker can paint you as unreliable and you'll be finished, never get a job. Are you taking this seriously?"

"Yes."

"But seriously enough?"

I was taking it seriously enough, plenty enough.

"I'll never eat lunch in this town again, right?"

"Now," Jay said, "I could get into a pissing war on your behalf, my newspaper against his. There hasn't been much of this in this town for quite some time."

"I know."

"Except that I'm walking on tender legs over at the *Independent*. I don't have the clout I once had, because you know why..."

"I know why."

"Ben Hawkins can only do so much to watch my back. But here's what's going on."

"More?"

"Gruberman knows all about your little escapade with Katrina Interlante."

"I'm not surprised. He's got his spooks everywhere."

"That's right," said Jay. "Don't trust anybody, including Carlos Loomis."

"I've begun to suspect," I said.

"Well suspect this...he's got Loomis on his payroll now."

"That *is* a surprise," I said. "But why?"

"One, to have a standby in case you don't come through on that dreck of a documentary he wants. He's picked Loomis as your backup."

"You know this?"

"I've got sources...right into his newsroom. We have quite a chatty grapevine."

"So that's one," I said. "Is there a two?"

"Back to Katrina," Jay said. "How do you feel about her?"

"I may be in love with her."

"What about Barbara?"

"I may be in love with her, too," I said.

"Back to Katrina."

"Yes, back to Katrina."

"Miles Korwin," Jay said.

"The son of a bitch critic who's been stalking her?"

"Do you know whose paper he writes for?" Jay said.

"Don't tell me."

"Gruberman owns *The Express*, and online that particular gossip tabloid gets a millions hits a day."

I was starting to get the picture.

"He could destroy her."

Yes, I was beginning to get the picture.

Adolf could destroy me in his *Manhattan Voice* and at the same time destroy Katrina in his *Express*.

"Good sleuthing, Jay."

"Not for nothing was I an investigative reporter. How much are you into him?"

"Half a million."

"Ouch."

"It adds up," I said.

"I'm sure you have racing stories."

"I was this close," I said.

"Never mind the details."

"Right. We all have the stories and they're always the same."

"Playing the horses won't get you back, as we can see."

True, neither of us here at the OTB was winning big. We were winning, but not big, certainly not in big enough numbers for Adolf Gruberman.

"Were you ever going to make that film?"

"No. But I shot some scenes to make him happy."

"Did he see them?" asked Jay.

"Yes and he was thrilled."

"I'm sure you had no trouble getting actors," said Jay.

"Are you kidding? They're still coming out of the woodwork. I could probably get eighty percent of your staff to volunteer."

"Don't get me started," said Jay.

"I can't imagine what you go through."

"Times have changed."

"I don't think so," I said.

"Agreed."

"Guess I'll have to do something."

"Never that documentary," Jay said. "Please."

"Give me more credit than that, Jay. I'd rather do porn."

"Well that would be porn."

"Political porn," I said.

"Tell me all that money didn't go to the horses."

"Craps helped."

Jay laughed.

"I never got in as deep as you," Jay said, and then reflected. "Well, not on the gambling."

"A woman is your vice."

"What do you think of her?"

"She's a knockout."

"Worth the trouble?"

"Probably not," I said.

"Wish I could be so level-headed," Jay said.

"I can be wonderfully level-headed when it comes to someone else, namely you at the moment."

We went to the bar for a drink before the next race. We were not at this time too much into the horses. We did not meet up often enough. We crossed paths here in New York and three times in the Middle East covering wars in and around Israel. We were there for Gaza, twice, and once for Lebanon. We had not planned it that way but that was how it turned out. Jay was doing combat reporting and I was doing combat filming. As editor in chief, he did not have to be there, but he liked to say that he wouldn't let any reporter do what he wouldn't do.

Besides, the reporting that came through from his men and women in the field was too often lopsided and biased, so that he had no recourse but to see for himself. Too many of them left town opinionated to begin with and it showed in their dispatches. They had a single point of view and held to it from beginning to end. Some of them he brought back and got them started again on obits.

His finest foreign correspondent had been captured by the terrorists and beheaded. He'd gone out there to exchange himself, but it was too late. His newsroom was in an uproar as to what to name the terrorists, most going for the terms "militants" or "fighters" or even "freedom fighters," while he stuck to "terrorists" and had won the day, until he lost. He lost Ben Hawkins, the publisher, who now had to answer to his sheiks.

Jay was in trouble all around and I had the feeling that he wanted to get cut loose. He wouldn't quit. Journalism was too dear to him to do that and he still had stories to cover and a newsroom to manage and the facts to present for a public that was being manipulated by messengers bringing false information. He was weary of it all, as was the public itself. Only 13 percent of the American people believed what they were being told. Jay placed part of the problem at the feet of *60 Minutes*, which operated its journalism upon the concept of "tell them a story."

When you told a story you fashioned it like a fairytale, providing a beginning, a middle and an end and you created the hero against the villain, and these heroes and villains answered and conformed to your own political and personal beliefs, so that indeed you were telling a story, but not necessarily the truth, and in fact as often as not you were twisting the truth.

Another of his foreign correspondents had been raped in Cairo while covering a demonstration and that had to be covered up to protect the politics.

Jay had tried to fight this, battler that he was, and earlier he would have won, but again he lost.

"When did it turn?" I asked.

"Probably with Woodward and Bernstein when it was no longer about reporting but about making the world a better place."

"The idealists took over."

"Exactly," he said.

At a cost of $280 I boxed my four numbers and hit an exacta, but without much of a profit.

Chapter 29

Katrina phoned to ask if I'd read the latest from Miles Korwin.

"No, and I never read him anyway and neither should you," I said.

Korwin had planted a terrible item about her.

I told her this would have to wait. I had urgent business.

"Please call when you can, or come, please. It has begun," she said.

"What has begun?"

"I can't explain this quickly."

"I'll call you as soon as I can."

"I would love for you to come over."

"We'll talk," I said.

"Have you been loving me?"

I said yes, but I wasn't so sure anymore. There was Hollywood love and there was real love and Katrina was Hollywood.

"Just one more day," she said and hung up, and I did not know what to make of this, either.

Chapter 30

The urgent business was a surprise invitation from a renegade rabbi. Rabbi Saul was a troublemaker, a rebel, a nonconformist, an outcast from the traditional ranks of the rabbinate. He was too liberal, too progressive, too rational, and even, in a number of instances, he disputed the sages of the past. He'd been properly and legitimately ordained from the Reform seminary in Cincinnati, and no one doubted his greatness as a thinker and writer. He was a genius, but his alleged apostasy was too much for his peers.

He'd been dismissed from his congregation somewhere in Baltimore for being so daringly outspoken...even among fellow reformists.

He was a man with a slight build, short, fit, tanned, and good-looking. He was unmarried and was not keen on observing strict dietary laws.

But still, he was a rabbi, and I seldom got along with rabbis.

We met at his study in Brooklyn.

"I've seen all your documentaries and I am impressed," he said, as a start, and a good start.

I thanked him.

"Have you heard about me?" he asked.

I said yes, that there was always something new about him from his detractors.

"So you know that I've been excommunicated."

"Yes, but I didn't know such things were still done."

The final nail was his *Letter to the Chief Rabbis of Israel*, where he blamed them for being too parochial, as opposed to popes Benedict XVI and John Paul II, each of whom inspired their own flock while reaching out to all faiths, as meanwhile Israel's chief religious leaders remained stubborn within their own orthodoxies and failed to inspire.

"So you know that I'm the Crazy Rabbi."

"I've heard that said, yes."

"So you know that I am not traditionally religious."

"I did not know that," I said.

He laughed. "I'm trying to get off cheeseburgers."

"Really," I said, really astonished.

His father had been an Orthodox rabbi.

"He would not have approved," Rabbi Saul said.

"I can imagine," I said.

"But he forgave me before he died."

Forgiveness again.

"So I guess you want to know why I called this meeting?"

"Of course."

As it unfolded, word was out that I was doing an anti-Semitic documentary.

"Can this be true?" the rabbi asked.

I was stumped. Do I tell him the truth, that I had made this deal with Adolf Gruberman on false pretenses and that I had no intention of going through with that blood libel? Do I tell him that I had already taken half a million dollars from that man and that most of it was already gone to the horses? He was a renegade all right, this rabbi, he ate cheeseburgers, but he was still a rabbi.

"Can I ask what brings this up?" I asked.

He'd been approached by Leaders of America's Christian Zionist movement who were about to denounce me if I went ahead and produced such a film.

"There are 80 million Christian Zionists in this country," the rabbi said, "people like Pat Robertson, and they are dismayed."

"This is a work in progress," I said, still unsure of my footing. Should I tell? What would he think of me if I came clean?

What would I think of myself if I came clean?

"Believe me," he said, "I know what it feels like to be an outcast. It is not a pretty thing."

"I understand."

"I don't think you do. You cannot imagine what it's like to be cut off from your people."

"If you mean the Jewish people, I am not quite Jewish."

"But your father is Jewish and that is close enough."

"True."

"You become a pariah," he said, "when you step out too far. Are you prepared for the consequences?"

"As I said..."

"Yes, yes, a work in progress, but already your name is being stained. Have you thought of your reputation?"

I said yes of course, but I said nothing about the gambling that made me so susceptible to the attraction of easy loot.

Right here, in the company of a rabbi, his library filled with religious texts, including the Five Books of Moses, I was stunned into quivers for what I had done.

Had I sinned a great sin?

Hell, I was a thief, but I would be no thief if I actually went ahead and finished it for Adolf. Why then I'd be no thief but a certified anti-Semite.

"Have you thought of your parents and what this could do to them? Your father?"

"He has his own reputation," I said.

"But he shares your name."

I'd be dragging him through the mud.

"This could be hurtful," the rabbi said, "unless of course you don't care."

"Excuse me?"

"Unless, that is, you share Gruberman's point of view."

"Of course not."

"As someone who is out of favor himself, believe me, I am not here to judge," the rabbi said. "I may be curious as to your motives."

Yes, my motives.

"I'm afraid my reasons are quite personal," I said.

"Yes, we all have to answer to ourselves eventually."

"Were you asked to speak to me?"

"Oh yes, and oddly enough, not by my fellow Jews, but as I said, by a number of Christian Zionists. They can't seem to understand why Jews are so quick to take up for the other side, these days especially. If you remember your Bible, we have had contrary sons throughout our history. But seldom as much as today. It has reached epidemic proportions and this baffles Christian Zionists. They come to rescue us from ourselves."

He offered me a brandy and said, "I have had my own spats with the Jewish State, but there is a line that should not be crossed."

I waited.

"We may get particular here and there, that is my sin, so to speak, but we should be careful not to denounce the land and its people."

"I have no intention of doing that," I assured him.

"Oh?"

"I do know the man he is, Gruberman, and you do know his first name is Adolf."

"Yes, odd."

"He could not possibly have been given that name at birth."

"He chose it?" the rabbi asked.

"Just a guess."

"Why not simply call himself Hitler?"

"Why not?"

"I don't know the man," said the rabbi, "but I know what he's done and what he can do. Are you under some kind of threat?"

I thought about this.

"Something like that," I said.

"Aha. Now we're getting close to something. Is this something for the police?"

"No, it's just between me and him."

"Aha. But you can't tell."

"Maybe some day I will," I said.

"Is your life at risk?"

"Possibly."

"Is there a reason why he picked you, aside from your excellence in film?"

This *much* I could tell him.

"He wants me to marry his daughter."

"But you're married."

"Separated."

"I know your father, you know."

"No I didn't know."

"I serve as chaplain to some nursing homes. Your dad is not in great shape."

I asked him if he had any suggestions.

He sighed. "Nursing homes – what can I say?"

"I would get them out of there if someone could find me a better place."

He gave it some thought. "If I can think of something, I'll let you know. Have you met the man who runs the place?"

"Charles Kessinger, oh yes."

"Something fishy," said the rabbi.

"Dad thinks there's a cult going on."

"Does he know your plans with that man?"

"Adolf?" I said.

"Yes, Adolf. Indeed, Adolf."

"Yes, Dad knows."

"Is he okay with what you have in mind?"

"I think he is, but..."

But Dad did not know how much money I had taken from Adolf. He knew I had taken some, maybe a few thousand dollars, but he'd be floored if he knew the full amount. No, he would not be happy to find out that I'd taken half a million from Adolf, no matter what I had in mind. He even encouraged me to play the man for a sucker, Adolf, but not to that extent.

I was in over my head, and wished that I could spill the beans to Rabbi Saul, who was not my image of a rabbi, but as a guy who'd be okay at the track. He was doing his job, asking questions. He was not judging, and for that I was grateful, and I especially liked the self-deprecating part about him. He was an outcast himself, and so he knew one when he saw one.

He showed me letters and even articles that denounced him as a turncoat and as a traitor.

"That's what you can expect," he said.

"I know."

"King Solomon taught that a good name is worth more than silver and gold."

"I get the point."

That was Jay Garfield who always reminded me that Adolf did not kill by bullets, but by ink.

"I'm told that you have already shot some footage," the rabbi said.

"Odds and ends."

"Did you have trouble finding people to participate?"

"Rabbi, they came at me in droves, amateurs and professionals, and they're still coming."

"Why am I not surprised," said Rabbi Saul.

He named a number of universities where he gives lectures.

"You wouldn't believe what I see and what I hear," he said.

"Anti-Semitism?"

"Oh yes. Jewish students are in danger, in danger for their lives."

"Even Harvard," I said.

"Especially Harvard," he said.

I still felt like telling him the truth.

"That picture will never get made," I said. "Not by me."

Chapter 31

But by Carlos Loomis.

Carlos was back at his studio in Margate and I was finishing up some shooting for him in Greenwich Village. I asked Gladys if she had my check.

"Carlos has it in Margate," she said.

"That's unusual."

"Not my problem."

Kids today...

I phoned Carlos and he said, yes, he forgot, but come on over to Margate because we had to talk anyway.

So anyway I took myself to Margate. Carlos was at his desk and on the phone and something told me he was on the phone with Adolf.

The conversation went like this from his end:

"There won't be a problem telling him."

"That's right. He's had plenty of time."

"I agree. That's a bad habit."

"How much? That's a small fortune."

"No, he's not the kind to cause a scene."

"Right, just leave it to me."

Then he was off the phone and asked me to wait. He had to talk to a few people out in the lobby.

The son of a bitch.

Unless I heard wrong.

Fortunately I didn't need this job. Not really. But word would get around that I'd been fired. This was never good.

He wouldn't have to tell. This business had ears.

Carlos came back and said, "Are you happy with your work?"

"You're firing me?"

"Did I say that?" he asked.

"I'm asking, yes or no?"

"No ultimatums, please."

"Yes or no."

"Okay, here's the deal. We're running out of money. As you know, the funds keep drying up."

"Okay."

"So how would you feel about working, you know, as a volunteer?"

"A volunteer."

"You know, until the money comes through."

"What money?"

"There's always money. You should know that, Gil."

Oh I see.

"Who else is volunteering?"

Carlos gave it that long grin.

"The interns, of course."

There were three interns.

"So this makes me an intern."

"I'm not saying that," he said.

"How about this?"

"Okay."

"Just a suggestion, I mean as an alternative."

"I just told you we have no money."

"This won't take any money," I said.

"Okay, shoot."

"How about this..."

His phone buzzed and he talked and chuckled for a while.

Then: "Okay, but I'm telling you there is no money."

"I'm telling you my suggestions won't need money."

"I'm always open to suggestions," Carlos said.

"How about you stick your thumb up your ass and go fuck yourself."

Chapter 32

Katrina was in town and staying with her sister in Brooklyn. I didn't know she had a sister and, as it was, I didn't know Katrina. Maybe I didn't take her seriously enough because she was an actress, and worse, Hollywood! Was anything real over there – *anything*? Her sister told me that she had tried to take her life, not about me specifically, but about other business.

I suggested that she quit committing suicide or else one day she could find herself dead.

"My sister exaggerates," she said. "I overdosed. It was an accident."

We were some place having coffee and bagels.

Yes, I had seen the items online and in the tabloids and even in the broadsheets, that she was "box office poison." A term like that had not been used since Joan Crawford.

"Only my last picture failed," she said.

Partly true. Her two pictures before that had not failed but had not sizzled, either. She was thinking of moving to New York, starting all over again.

The theater, maybe.

"Or, you could come to terms with Drake Goldsmith."

I had been on the phone to him several times, but he refused to change his mind on the casting.

"There are no terms to discuss," I told her.

Maybe it happens once they leave the garden that nourishes them...here in New York she wasn't the same.

We were talking as if nothing had happened between us.

"I feel that the part was made for me," she said, about the Joan character.

"I agree, but if you can't get Drake to change his mind, how can I?"

She lowered her eyes and stayed quiet.

"He offered me a part," she said.

"Well that's good."

"Do I have to tell you this?"

"What?"

"But they turned me down."

"Who did?"

"Wilson."

"The director?"

"The director."

She had appealed to Drake, but Drake supported Wilson.

"He said he could not interfere."

"So that's how it goes," I said.

"That's how it goes."

She knew I had gotten fired.

"No, I quit."

"That's not what they say."

"What are you suggesting?" I asked.

"Can somebody be behind all this?"

"What do you mean?"

"We both seem out of luck, and at the same time," she said.

I gave this some thought. Conspiracy?

"I don't believe in conspiracies," I said.

"I never did, but now I wonder. People do know about you and me, you know."

"I know."

"Nothing strikes you as strange?"

I did not want to think what I was thinking.

"Out with it," I said.

"Okay, rumors about you, rumors about me – my God, box office poison! – and you can't see a connection?"

Were we into Adolf Gruberman territory? I told her all about him – everything!

"Oh my God! Don't you see?"

I told her that I was afraid it could come to this, if conspiracy was what this was.

"But I'm not ready to draw this conclusion. Do you really believe he has connections in Hollywood?" I asked.

"That man has connections everywhere, from what I hear. Isn't he the fourth richest man in the world?"

Yes he is. Yes he is. Indeed he is.

"He can buy the studio, along with Goldsmith – and is his name really Adolf?"

"Absolutely," I said.

"Why would a man do this to himself?"

"Beats me," I said.

"He's Jewish, isn't he?"

"Not anymore."

"Aha. I don't need to guess what religion he convert-ed to," she said.

"Just use your imagination."

"So he's ruining you, and he's ruining me, and we're just sitting here talking," she said.

"He wants something from me."

"So I heard, but I don't know the details," she said.

"Better you don't."

"Why?"

"You'd think less of me."

"Never. I still love you, you know. Do you still love me?"

"Aha," I said.

Chapter 33

I was in the racing room at the casino and was having the best day in years. I had given up playing my numbers and went back to strict scientific handicapping. This was lady luck making it up to me. Every finish by a nose went my way. If only I could package this. It was a good day and it got better when Black Dude Andre came over. He had spare tickets for the Kentucky Derby. "They're yours," he said.

The big race was still weeks away, but I was excited and counted off the days. I bought every racing chart I could find on each of the 12 horses that had already been chosen to run. I was determined to make this my day of days. First I'd pick the winner and everything would fall into place from there, the exacta, the trifecta, and the super trifecta. I would study and handicap as never before. I also wanted to be there for the festivities. I made plane reservations well in advance.

I tried to be calculated meanwhile on the races I bet locally in order to save up for the Derby. I figured to invest $10,000 in the Derby. Meantime to preserve my cash here at the New York tracks, I even bet place and show, along with win, of course. I played it safe. I played it safe and did all right, nothing fancy, but okay. I seldom went home losers.

I managed to shut everything out. I went to the races every day. Dark days were a nightmare, so I played the tables and didn't do too bad. I tried some blackjack; couldn't figure out why people played that game. You invested only to get your money back. So I stopped. Craps was much more like gambling, so that's what I played, but carefully. This was where you could lose your shirt.

I visited some friends in the backstretch just to be hanging around the horses, the trainers, the jockeys, the grooms. They had information but it was seldom reliable, but it was still good to be around them instead of being suffocated within the synthetics of all those racing rooms. All around people were asking, "Who ya like in the Derby?" My kind of talk.

Horseracing was my address.

There was only so much to do about all the problems that I faced from behind and up front. Mostly there was nothing to be done. Somehow, gambling solved everything. You were sheltered. You entered a different zone, another dimension. You couldn't be touched – and now I had a new system, and no, not a new gambling system, but a new way of life.

These days I refused to bring my cell phone with me. Why should I – why should anyone – be so constantly accessible? How about some privacy? There used to be a time for everything, a time to laugh, a time to cry, a time to love, a time to hate, a time for peace, a time for war, a time to sleep, a time to gamble, but all that stopped with technology gone wild, so that you had to keep answering the phone no matter where you were and there was no stopping a thousand intrusions into your life.

So I also kept the phone dark, often enough, when I was out or when I was in. I reckoned that I didn't make much difference anyway. The world would go on without me whether I answered the phone or not. Was anything really that urgent? Weren't there other people who could attend to this or that emergency? I was just one member of the whole shebang, and from beginning to end; each man is an island unto himself.

I found myself sleeping more than usual. Not that I was so tired, just that I had made up my mind to keep to myself. I found that it was best not to get involved with people, strangers and even friends, especially friends. Involvement so often spelled trouble. There was always a favor you failed to recompense, a birthday you forgot – and people kept score. The more friends a man has the more likely he is to make enemies.

I was beginning to forget what it was that I was pursuing – and what's the rush? We all want something, but I couldn't remember what I wanted. There were days when I left the track not remembering, only a few hours later, whether I had won or lost, for all the rooting and heaving I had done during the races. I was getting philosophical, or maybe I was gaining some wisdom, if only by accident, that win or lose, we all end up together at the same finish line.

Not that I was getting depressed, necessarily; only that I'd found a sphere of peace. Or maybe not. I wasn't sure. Maybe I was depressed. I took note of this when on a particular day... when again I was hot... I collected $12,420 on a fine trifecta, and hardly cared. I simply could not figure out what difference it made, about anything. Really – what?

I knew people who thought they were masters of the universe after a big win. They were all over the place, especially at poker. They really felt impregnable. For them, that good hand that wiped the table, this meant that they had conquered man and fate. I never had that sensation or felt that degree of satisfaction. But those were the professionals, and I was not a professional gambler, compulsive maybe, but not professional. I had other businesses. I knew this. This was what I knew. I could never quit the gambling.

In the beginning, after a bad day, I would tell myself "never again." But there I was, back again. Soon I realized that I was hooked.

I still had trouble with my teeth. I was at the dentist's about once every two weeks, and usually for an emergency. Old Dr. Herbert Kling used to just do this and that and took care of me without much talk or comment. He'd never give it a name even if it were a canker or something. He knew that names scared people. So he'd just say, "There's a swelling. We'll take care of it, don't worry." Then his son James took over and he was much more talkative and more polite and more pleasant than his father and quite a fucking bastard. He gave everything a name, by the book, and refused to see you for an emergency. He blamed you for taking so long before scheduling a visit, for letting a problem get out of hand, and he insisted on a system of "complete care" and if you did not comply you were out of luck. He said, "You're dealing with me now. Not my father." That's when I switched.

This too was not so unusual, to find people who were so awfully nice to likewise be fucking bastards.

"Hello," I finally said.

"It's your mother," said Barbara – whose calls and messages I had also been avoiding.

I had been avoiding the computer all that time, for that entire period, and simply kept hitting delete as often as I hit mute for the TV. I deleted all those emails, and some may have been important, but it felt good. I would not be a slave to importance. Importance would have to do without me. I had other plans, or rather no plans, except for the business at hand, which was nailing the Kentucky Derby, which was now only weeks away.

But I just knew that something had to come along. Something always comes along.

What to do about family, a family you love? What to do about a woman you love, but a woman who cheated on you? The worst of it was that Barbara was easy to love; that is, she was likeable. She was a good person. Oh she could be witty and snappy and sophisticated, but she was a girl of Manhattan, after all. She had to do right by her sisters. She could not let them down by being "sweet."

I noticed that the more I distanced myself from her, the closer she got to my parents. It took no Einstein or Freud to figure that out. I had set aside some of her emails where she spoke of making a fresh start. That could even be exciting and sexy. Well yes, but you had to be in the mood and I was not in the mood, not yet. I wondered if I ever would be.

I wondered if I could ever find the strength to forgive her. Wasn't that the man's role – to cheat?

At the one or two GA sessions I attended this woman got up and blamed everything on men – men do the gambling and the boozing and the cheating and the fighting and the farting. I could only agree. It is all our fault. We are the worst of the species. Put the blame on us for all the faults throughout the world, beginning at home. We can't even get it straight about how to behave within the family. Spousal abuse was all over the place and I had produced and directed a documentary on the topic, though I do not think anything has changed, and despite the good GA does, no one has stopped compulsive gambling, except for an individual here and there, and in fact the problem has gotten worse. Now there are slot machines from state to state and women are suckers for the slots, and for the lotteries. That used to be a male preserve, gambling. So what was she doing there, Anna G.? She was there for the cure of her husband who had crashed his car into the garage door after losing a daily double...and I was not the only one who had tried to reach Aqueduct during a blizzard. Though it may have been some other tracks for my fellow degenerates. One guy had tried the entire tri-state circuit when it was impossible to drive.

But do women do this? Do women cheat enough to fall into degeneracy? Do women cheat? My woman did.

"I'll be right over," I said.

I had been at the track having fun with Black Dude Andre when the call came. He was telling about his years on the police force.

You should do a documentary on that, he said.

People always said that.

There's no gratitude. You help them you save them, and they don't give a shit. This one kid, from Columbia – the university – I answered an alarm. He was getting mugged. I got there just in time. One more minute and he'd have been a dead man. He tells me, he says that he doesn't like cops. So I told him. I said next time you need help call your professor, punk.

Andre said that after years on the beat you simply lose your faith in people.

If it was me on that ship, I'd have jumped ship just like that Italian captain did on that Italian liner. So long suckers, good luck. I'm going home. Got pussy waiting.

Well, it wasn't my mother; it was my father who'd been taken in for "evaluation." Mom had resorted to Barbara when she couldn't reach me. For some reason I took my time driving over. I knew what to expect and if it was something different I didn't want to know about it either. How long now had I promised to get them out but didn't? How much of this was my fault?

First Barbara and I met for coffee at some Dunkin Donuts not far from Kessinger's Communal Living Estates for 55-plus. That was the problem. Mom and Dad were 55-plus. There was no getting around that fact, or the fact that we – as a civilized civilization – did not know what to do with such people. We treated them like lepers or invaders. We developed medicines to keep people alive, but after that we turned our backs on *plus-55*.

So here come missionaries like Charles Kessinger, ready to pounce and pick up the pieces. They build grand estates that are ready-made for brochures and postcards. Everything is about "ideal living for seniors." Only it is not so ideal, and some of them have other plans, like creating conditions that require their captives to adapt to different, sometimes strange, customs.

"They claim he had another spell," said Barbara, "but they're still unsure if it's a stroke or part of his Alzheimer's."

"They claim? You saw him?"

"I did, but I didn't see anything unusual about him, but I'm not a doctor."

"Where's he now?"

"Still in their hospital."

"How about my mother. Never mind. I don't have to ask."

We went over to the hospital.

The nurse knocked on the door.

"Your son is here," she said.

"That's why *I'm* here," said Dad.

He was laughing when we went in.

"Couldn't resist that line," he said, ever the writer.

"So what happened?" I asked.

"Which version do you want?"

Dad always said that there's a short version and a long version to every story.

"Short," I said.

"By the way," he said, "what's with you two? Why don't you get married or something?"

"We are married," said Barbara.

"You know what I'm talking about, and I didn't misspeak because I'm decrepit."

"So what happened?"

"They're experimenting on me. Did you see Dr. Mengele?"

Dr. Mengele was Auschwitz's *Angel of Death*.

We had spoken to one of the doctors who said they were indeed taking tests, but so far nothing was coming up conclusive.

His name was not Dr. Mengele, it was Peters, but he was not nice.

"What did he say, Mengele?"

"Peters, Mr. Gilels," said Barbara. "They still want you in for observation."

"Then they send you to the starvation room..."

"The dieting room, Dad."

"THE STARVATION ROOM."

"Dad."

"The purpose is to get you to die. When are you going to believe me?"

What was true was this; nobody around this place was nice. The rudeness seemed purposeful.

"They run some sort of a religion around here," said Dad.

"Nothing wrong with that," I said stupidly.

"Well it's no religion I know of, except what they practiced in Sodom."

In Sodom there was no place for compassion and people who were compassionate were stoned to death.

"Is that what you're saying?" asked Barbara.

"That's what I've *been* saying."

True, and Dad's instincts were not to be taken lightly.

"I developed a bit of a stammer," said Dad.

"You always had a bit of a stammer," I said.

"Exactly. Well it was noticed in their goddamn work room."

"Someone snitched on you?" asked Barbara.

"Those are the rules. You're expected to snitch. That used to be known as white terror, when you couldn't trust anybody."

"Then?" I said.

"Then they came for me, just as you see it in the movies."

"Men in white coats?"

"Blue coats. They came to the door and arrested me....for stammering."

"They'd say they were giving you medical attention," I said.

"They look for any excuse to put you in the starvation room. Nobody gets out of there alive."

I wondered if this could be proven. He could be right.

"There is nothing wrong with me," Dad said. "Do I look sick? Do I sound sick?"

No he didn't.

"Do you know who snitched on you?"

"One of the residents. I think I know who it is, but what difference does it make? They're all the same. Have you noticed how they're all the same?"

Of this there was no doubt. They were all the same, sickly, emaciated, unsmiling and unpleasant.

"She whispered something to the supervisor. They don't remove you right on the spot. They don't want to alarm the other residents."

So they waited for him to get back to his bungalow and then took him.

But there was more. Mom told us that part when we got to the bungalow.

"They handcuffed him," Mom said.

"What!"

"They said he was putting up a struggle, and perhaps he was."

Mom, as it turned out, had been sedated, and there was still a nurse in her room, so we had to speak carefully.

"He went mad when they came for him."

Even that sounded sinister – *they came for him.*

"Like how?"

"The usual protests, and he refused to go with them. So they restrained him."

"Did you notice anything wrong with him?"

"In his condition it goes back and forth, but no, nothing like a stroke."

"But they would say..."

"That's the point. They argue that at any sign of illness it's their duty...oh maybe they're right."

That was the point. Maybe they were right.

"Have you gone over?"

"Your father won't let me."

"What?" said Barbara.

"He's afraid if I show up they'll take me, too. Your dad is not paranoid, Gil." She started to weep. "Do you know the great man he was – *is?*"

"We'll get him out," Barbara said.

"But suppose he *is* having a stroke? Suppose they know what they're doing? Suppose they really do care about us?"

"I feel terrible," I said, sitting down or rather collapsing in a chair.

Mom came over to run her fingers through my hair, like it was when we were young. Yes, once upon a time she was young.

Barbara started crying, heavy sobs.

"Please don't put this on yourself, Gil," said Mom. "We tried everything else."

"But did we try enough?"

"They were all the same," said Mom, "and most of them were even worse."

"Dad would argue the point."

"Well you know your father. He has a writer's imagination."

"Only he isn't imagining this."

"You know," she brightened, "he does have a nursing home scene in one of his novels."

I laughed. "Now he'll have another one."

"He has been busy at the typewriter. Yes, he could be writing about this very place."

We went to see Charles Kessinger.

"Do you have an appointment?"

Barbara explained the situation.

"He's busy on his sermon."

"We also have a sermon," I said.

"One moment."

We waited.

There was another young couple in the waiting room.

"Does this place give you the creeps?" the lady said.

"Do you know their motto?" the man said.

Not exactly their motto, but the refrain went like this: *Everyone needs a pass to leave and nobody gets a pass.*

"Once you're in, you're in," said the man.

I asked why they were waiting for Kessinger.

"I had my mom in here," said the lady, "and she died. I have papers to fill out. You will, too, when the time comes."

We started comparing nursing homes.

"They're all the same," said the husband.

"We tried everything," said the wife.

"So did we," said Barbara.

"So these are the glories of growing old?" said the husband.

"We took her out of here at one point," said the wife, "and took her to a nursing home that a month later was shut down for elder abuse."

"Physical abuse," said the husband, "which they don't do over here. But they do everything else, and this may be even worse."

"Have you seen how weird all the people look?" said the wife.

"My dad thinks they're being starved."

"He may be on to something," said the husband.

"Mom was terribly emaciated toward the end. They said she refused to eat. Have you smelled their food in the diet room? Would you eat that crap?"

Yes, I had smelled the food, and yes, it was crap.

"There seem to be no options," said the husband.

Chapter 34

"Blessings," said Charles Kessinger, "and your father has been released. The results came back negative."

That was fast.

I asked him about the handcuffs.

"That's for the safety of our residents when we fear they may lose control. Have you visited our church?"

I asked him again about the handcuffs.

"Safety above all," he said. "We could be held liable if something were to go wrong during transport."

I did not much care for the word *transport*.

Barbara asked about the snitching.

Kessinger turned righteous.

"That is part of our system of control. Our residents need to be watched and monitored. It's for their own good."

I asked him if he knew his Bible.

"We run our lives and we run this entire community through the precepts of the Bible. I happen to be an ordained minister."

I asked if he was aware of the Bible's prohibition against talebearing, as per Leviticus.

He gave this some thought.

"Tattling is a sin according to my Bible," I said.

He was still thinking.

"You encourage this?" asked Barbara. "Really?"

"Perhaps our view of the Bible differs from yours," Kessinger said.

"Different how?" Barbara said.

Kessinger had to excuse himself for a few moments to attend to business outside his office.

"Do you see how evasive he is?" said Barbara. "He's got a double meaning for everything."

"He anticipates every question," I said.

"And never gives a straight answer."

"But everything makes sense, in a strange sort of way."

"Right, in a strange sort of way."

Kessinger came back. "That's why I invite you to our church."

I asked him how his views on the Bible differed.

"We have our own practices and our own liturgies, all for the betterment of our patients, and frankly, for the betterment of mankind."

"Sir, you mean you have your own interpretations?"

He let that sit.

"Our interpretations are meant to deal with the world as it is, not as it should be," he finally said.

"What about the Ten Commandments?" asked Barbara.

"That too is open to interpretation."

"Are you saying you operate from a different set of ethics?" asked Barbara.

"We keep an open mind," said Kessinger.

I asked if his *religion* stuck to *Love Thy Neighbor as Thyself?*

Here he got somewhat excited. "That is a standard impossible to fulfill," he said. "We deal with facts on the ground, not with the ideals of heaven."

"Wait a minute," I said. "In other words you do not believe in loving your neighbor as yourself."

"We understand love differently," he said. "You should attend our services."

"Differently," said Barbara.

"Love cannot be imposed," he said.

"Are you suggesting hatred in place of love?"

"Of course not," he said, "only to teach, according to our faith, that each man is in it alone and should expect no favors."

Each man is in it alone and should expect no favors.

That, as I was to learn later from his sermons, was the credo of the Faith of St. Iris.

Each man is in it alone and should expect no favors.

Well now, that certainly was a new kind of religion. Or maybe not.

"That's positively heathen," said Barbara.

"On the contrary. It is positively Biblical."

"Well then," I said. "We read different Bibles, you and I."

"How would you deal with the elderly?" he asked, still calm and preacher-like.

"Not like this," I said.

"You children come in here and expect miracles. You send us your aged, people who can't fend for themselves, and you ask us, you expect us to provide them with the same world they left behind – and indeed that is precisely what we do, though not according to your lights. You expect us to baby them and to look after them with unconditional affection. But that is not how it works in the world they left behind – nor is that how it will work in the world that is still ahead. In that world, the world of the future, there will be no compassion, no love of the widow or the orphan or the stranger; dog eat dog. We teach, we preach no favors asked, no favors given, and thus we train our residents to stand on their own two feet."

He reminded us that other homes for the aged allowed their people to idle away their years. Nothing was expected of them except to die.

"Yet here," he said, "we provide activities and training to prepare them for a brighter future."

Barbara and I shared a look – didn't he mean a *darker* future?

Each man is in it alone and should expect no favors.

I told him that if my father were ever handcuffed again, I'd go to the police.

He was still calm, far too calm.

"We are certified by the State," Kessinger said. "Everything we do is checked and double-checked. Inspectors are here once a month."

He dangled this.

"Remove your parents if you wish. Find them a better place, if you can."

He knew that we had tried that, without success. To remove my parents – first there'd be a $70,000 penalty for breaking the contract.

We went back to my parents' bungalow.

"Smooth operator, that Kessinger, right?" said my father.

"He has the edge," I said.

Mom kept busy in the kitchen. As Dad's desk was his place of refuge, so was the kitchen for Mom. She liked to pretend that nothing was troubling her, especially when things were at their worst. She had a powerful capacity to keep her pains to herself, to act nonplussed when the world around her was in turmoil. She was Dad's rock.

She acted according to her own private belief that *this too shall pass.*

"I feel terrible for putting you two kids through this," Dad said.

"We're not the ones hurting," Barbara said.

"Hah! Look at yourselves."

He preferred to drop the subject. He wanted to talk sports, books, movies – culture.

"I suppose I'd be a prude if I dissented from what's happing to our culture," he said. "On television, from the hour we can catch, anything goes. Sex is out in the open. The limits have been breached. I saw something the other day, on prime time, that was beyond belief. We're down at the crotch level. I suppose this makes me a prude, but when a civilization – well we know that civilizations get destroyed by decay within."

Barbara asked his views on homosexuality, which too was now in the open, along with same-sex marriage.

"Glad you asked. I happen to be writing on the subject and I've arrived at several conclusions. Which do you want, the short or the long?"

"The medium, Dad," I said.

"First, what do I care what people do in their own bedrooms, as long as nobody gets hurt. If it's consensual it's none of my business or anybody's business. Second, I take it from Fitzgerald that the test of a first-rate mind is the ability to function even when two opposing ideas are in conflict. So...my teaching has it that homosexuality is an abomination. I get that, but I also get it that some of the greatest people were gay; we even have relatives who are gay. Am I to shun my teaching? No. Am I to shun my loved ones? No. So I accept the fact. I accept the fact that in life not everything can be resolved, that we simply must continue to live with conflicts and not to expect to answer every question. In fact, we go on even as we know that, really, nothing in this life gets resolved." He paused. Obviously he was reciting something he had written or was going to write. "Or as you say, Gil – the investigation continues. Hah. I like that. The investigation continues."

He asked, and then I reminded him where I got that line.

"That's right," he said. "You covered the police beat when you wrote for that paper in New Jersey."

I walked over to Mom in the kitchen.

"He sounds like his old self, doesn't he?" she said.

"Not bad," I said. "What about you?"

"I manage."

"Is there anything I don't know?" I asked her.

"He still thinks they're trying to convert us to some sort of cult."

"And?"

"And I'm starting to believe him. What did Kessinger have to say?"

"He's got all the answers, Mom. He can't be cornered."

"His view of the world is too realistic for me," she said.

"More than that," I said.

"How so?"

"More than realistic, downright frightening," I said.

"What sort of religion encourages informers?" she asked.

"You mean you're being watched."

"Everybody. The supervisors, of course, do their own snooping. But even residents are told to report on their neighbors."

"Kessinger says it's all about safety."

"That's where it gets tricky. He has a point. But your father believes that we're being conditioned to believe in a world without mercy."

"What about you?"

"Your father and I – God love him – have never had the same outlook."

"I know that, Mom. That's what's made you an endurable couple."

She laughed, happily.

"If your dad had married someone like himself he'd have gone loopy a long time ago. Your dad has always seen the dark side of the moon, forever the pessimist, and always waiting for the other shoe to drop. He can be volcanic and, of course, moody. He can also be forgetful and eccentric. He is a writer, after all, and he has an artistic temperament. I have always been the optimist."

"I know that, Mom, and that's what saved him all these years."

"But if I were to come around to his thinking, so far as thinking the worst, then where do we go?"

She began to weep softly. I embraced her.

"Is that really the world," she said, "a world without love or mercy?"

"That's one man's opinion," I said about Kessinger.

"But is he wrong?"

"We call that a half-truth," I said.

"So it isn't an outright lie," said Mom, "and he sees it, he sees the world like that even for the future. What can we expect from you and our grandchildren?"

Barbara and I had been putting it off. But it was still part of our plans – or had been part of our plans.

"There will be grandchildren for us, won't there be?" said Mom.

I could not answer that one; not with us being separated, and not with me hanging on to the hurt.

Mom and Dad did not know what happened. They only knew that something had gone wrong. But Dad had suspected all along.

"But you have grandchildren," I said, mentioning my sister Karen and her fourth baby.

"You think that's the end?" said Mom.

We heard raised voices.

Dad was saying:

"I was not meant to grow old."

Barbara kept calming him down.

"I was not meant to be an old man, do you understand?"

"You are not an old man," Barbara kept saying.

"I was not prepared for this."

Chapter 35

I went straight to the racetrack to regain my footing and to forget my transgressions, my sins and my guilt. I had no answers except for the Daily Racing Form. There the charts made sense and there I could divine the future as no place else. Nothing but the horses ran true to form, certainly not the people who ran our lives. *Survival of the fittest* that man had said, if not in so many words – that terrible man and his terrible world.

He had created a model for the world of tomorrow – modeled after a page from the Bible, that page of Sodom.

Each man is in it alone and should expect no favors.

Hadn't my dad anticipated that? Yes he had, in his novel *The Voice in the Wind.* But not to this extent. He did see it coming, or something like this.

"Hey, no moping around here," said Black Dude Andre.

"That's not why we come to the races," said Jay Garfield.

"Crackerjack," said Andre.

"I know the owner," said Jay.

"I know the trainer," I said.

"Any word?" they both asked.

"Says he gave him a race last time," I said.

"So he should be shooting the works today," said Andre. "He's been going bad but I once made a ton of money on that horse."

"They play games," said Jay.

"Inside word from the groom is that the horse is not ready," I said.

"Trainer knows best," said Andre. "Some of that juice does wonders."

"I don't think he uses it," said Jay, still going over the charts.

"Look at him out there; looks like a milk horse. His ears aren't even pinned back. I don't like him. Not today," said Andre.

"His odds keep going up," said Jay.

"Never a good sign right before the race, when the smart money starts coming in. Even his connections don't like him," laughed Andre. "Like the hillbilly said when he kicked out his bride when he found out she was a virgin – if she ain't good enough for her own kin, she ain't good enough for me. Hah. If she ain't good enough for her own kin, she ain't good enough for me."

"I still think he's worth a small bet," said Jay, "just for the memories."

Crackerjack was an old horse that had failed as a stud so they brought him back to the races.

Jay had already sent Phil Crawford out to the Middle East to cover the war...where the battles had already cost the lives of 26 journalists within a month. Jay was in worse trouble than Phil. He had already lost his job as editor at the *Manhattan Independent* over the scandal, a love triangle that was now all over the news and that had cost Lyla Crawford her job as well. Each of them used to be *somebody*.

"You pass your trainer's license yet?" Andre asked Jay as we all sat there handicapping one minute and making our bets the next.

"I'm good to go," said Jay.

"You got newsprint in your blood," said Andre. "How you going to make the switch?"

"It's what I always wanted to do."

"Keep telling yourself that," said Andre. To me he said, "You nuts?"

I was putting $1,000 to win on Crackerjack.

"But you don't even like the horse," said Andre.

"He's going off 20 to one," said Jay.

"Still my horse," I said.

"Why do you always bet longshots?" said Andre.

"Because favorites never win, not for me."

"You're crazy," said Andre. "Why do you think they're called longshots, huh? They're called longshots because they never win."

"Never?" said Jay.

"You gonna try to make a living playing longshots?"

"I just did it," said Jay, talking about something else.

"You're both crazy," said Andre. "Favorites are favorites for a reason. Everything's ready for them to win. Longshots are a sucker's bet."

"Did all right for me," I said.

"How often?" asked Andre.

"More often than you think."

"Chalk wins 33 percent of the time. I'll take those odds any day. You just trying to lose, Gil."

"You know me better than that," I said.

"You're trying to lose, Gil. You used to play the favorites."

"Why handicap if you're just playing the board?" I said.

"Nothing wrong with playing the board. They're *telling* who's going to win."

"They tell me nothing."

"The odds on everything you do are stacked against you," said Andre. "Agreed?"

Jay and I both agreed.

"I'm talking about life," said Andre.

"Got that," I said.

"So here's the one place where you've got an edge, and you won't play the edge," said Andre. "Makes no sense."

"Some people like to take chances," said Jay, still talking about something else.

"Makes no sense," said Andre.

Crackerjack finished fourth. Andre collected on Seabird. Jay also lost.

Andre came back from the window a happy man. He bought drinks all around.

"Is this the life?" he said.

"This is the life," Jay said.

"Hey, Gil, is this the life?"

"This is the life, Andre."

"Let me tell you something. No, let me ask you something. Do you think racing is crooked?"

"Most times no," said Jay.

I told them both that for the purposes of making a film we once tried to fix a race, and couldn't. The horses refused to cooperate.

"Well," said Andre, "I do believe that some crookedness does go on, but that the least crooked place in the world is the racetrack. Everything else is a scam. The stock market is a scam, politics is a scam, religion is a scam, TV is a scam; it's all fixed and crooked. Can't trust NO BODY. The fix is in wherever you turn. Anybody want to argue the point?"

"Hey," said Jay, "you're talking to a newspaperman, okay, ex-newspaperman. I know what's fixed."

"What's fixed?" asked Andre.

"Like you said," said Jay.

"Everything, right?"

"Can't deny that," said Jay.

"What do you say, Hollywood?"

He liked to call me Hollywood. People know you make films – even if most of it is not in Hollywood – they still call you Hollywood.

"The fix is in," I said.

"Worst is religion," said Andre. "That's where they really got you bamboozled. More than half the world is bamboozled."

"No," said Jay. "There's nothing worse than politics."

"Let's call it a dead heat," I suggested.

"How many women did you have to take to bed to get where you are today?" said Andre, laughing.

"Yeah, it's a tough life," I said.

"Come on," said Andre. "Names. You never give us names."

"Can't remember them all," I said. "There've been so many."

"Don't touch Halle Berry. Did you touch Halle Berry?"

"Hmm."

"I think he did," said Jay.

"You fucked Halle Berry?"

"I think he did," said Jay.

"Did you?"

"Does five times count?" I said.

"You never touched Halle Berry. I know you didn't."

"How do you know?" I said.

"Tell me you did."

"I can't remember."

That cracked him up.

"Oh you'd remember. Oh you'd remember, all right."

Andre said racing is a metaphor for life.

"What's life?" asked Andre.

"Do we have to answer right this minute?" said Jay. "It took Socrates all his years to figure it out, and he still never figured it out."

"Philosophers got no clue," said Andre. "That guy Descartes, know what he said?"

"Cogito ergo sum," Jay explained.

"Wrong language," said Andre.

"Je pense donc je suis," I explained.

"Right," said Andre. "I think therefore I am. That's supposed to be the most important philosophical statement of all time and it's bullshit."

"You got something new and improved?" asked Jay.

"I play the horses therefore I am," explained Andre.

"Deep," I said.

"I'm a gambler therefore I am," said Andre, "and if that's not the answer, I'll give it to you straight."

"We're waiting," said Jay.

"Life is about separating the winners from the losers, and that's why gambling is a microcosm for everything. Some people win, some people lose."

"Life in a nutshell," I said.

"Not bad," said Jay.

"I meant to say metaphor," said Andre, "and I do believe people are born that way. Some people are born winners. Some people are born losers."

"That's fatalistic, Andre. You're dismissing free will," I said.

"No such thing," said Andre. "We're stuck with fate."

"What a terrible judgment," said Jay.

"I can look at a man's face," said Andre, "and tell you right away if the man's going to hit his points or seven out. That's terrible, I know. But it's life."

"So forget that Oprah shit, right?" said Jay.

"Forget loving yourself no matter who you are, if that's what you mean. I can think of a lot of people who don't deserve to be loved..."

"Or to love themselves," I added.

"Only a mother can love some of the people I know," said Andre, "and I'm not so sure about the mother."

After winning and losing I started getting messages on my iPhone, and I thought I had turned it off. The one from Katrina said – *we should get together before this is all over.* Well now, that was something to think about. Before what's all over? What should I feel guilty about now? I started to wonder why I had gotten myself into this in the first place, besides wanting to get into the pants of a Hollywood movie star.

Chapter 36

Adolf Gruberman was showing me around his news-room at another one of his publications, *The Manhattan Scoop*. Who knew what garbage was being scooped in and scooped out of this place? I saw a hundred people busy at work at their computers and on the phones, most of the business about gossip, celeb gossip. He traf-ficked in that and in everything else. He had the power of the press on his side; more like it the power of his money.

We settled into his office and he told me straight out that if I failed to produce, Carlos Loomis was waiting on board to finish what I had started.

Hadn't I figured as much? For all his high talk, Carlos was a sell-out.

I told Adolf that if he wanted me to keep on going he'd have to call off the dogs, specifically Miles, that dog.

"Miles does what Miles does," said Adolf. "I don't con-trol him. I don't tell him what to write."

"He's ruining Katrina Interlante."

"She's ruining herself, been ruining herself for years. You've seen her latest pictures?"

"None of them deserved what she got from Miles," I said.

"I don't interfere," Adolf said.

"Now you're going after me."

He ignored that and said that if I didn't finish the job soon, he'd want all the footage I'd already taken. He'd want it for Carlos.

The date he named coincided with the date of the Kentucky Derby.

"What happened to the money?" he asked.

"What money?"

"*What* money? I gave you another quarter million to go location scouting. *What* money?"

"That's exactly what I've been doing," I said, and it was true, in some measure...although I was doing it for another film I had in mind.

"You know we've already missed several film festivals. Dubai is already done."

Too bad about Dubai.

"I'll want it in time for Cannes," he said.

I asked him if he was sure a film like this would be right for Cannes.

"Why would they object?"

"Something so political?" I said.

"So make it less political," he said.

There was no way to fit anti-Semitism into something less political.

"This is a hard-hitting film," I said.

"What film? I see no film."

"Once it's done," I said.

"Well it is going to get done, if not you, somebody else."

"Carlos Loomis."

"Yes, and there are others who want a crack at this," he said.

He had as many producers and directors who were ready to jump in as I had actors, amateur and professional.

"But they won't be starting it from scratch. I will definitely want the footage you have already done," said Adolf.

"That's my work," I said.

"My money," he said.

"I won't give up my work," I said.

"I won't give up my money," he said.

I told him that I may need more money.

He did not explode as I thought he would. In fact he sat back and smiled. He knew something.

"To get your folks out of that home?"

How – well of course he'd know that since he knew everything. That's why he had a hundred people on the phones.

"That's personal," I said.

"No," he said, "once I give money to somebody his business becomes my business."

I told him that I did not appreciate the messages he kept sending me.

"What messages?" he said.

"The ones that show up in your gossip columns. What good would it do you to ruin me since we're in this together?"

"We are in nothing together," he said. "You are in this alone, and ruin you? I don't ruin people. I only let people ruin themselves."

He said so many people needed no help getting ruined.

"I have been very patient," he said. "That much you have to admit."

That much I had to admit.

"Too patient, my people tell me about myself, and from you I get no gratitude and I get no results and, so far, no film."

His phone rang and he spoke for a while.

"That was Helen," he said.

His daughter.

"I hope she's well," I said.

"She's dating someone very acceptable," he said. "How about you and Barbara?"

This is where I still had him. He wanted me for Helen. But – if I got back with Barbara, or if Helen really found somebody, I would be sunk.

Helen was still saving me.

I had met her only once or twice, but for some reason she had eyes for me.

"I heard about your father," Adolf said. "He was a great man."

"Still is," I said.

"What do you think of Dr. Kessinger?"

"I should know better than to ask how you know Dr. Kessinger."

He laughed.

"I make it my business to know. We run in the same circles, let's just say. Do you think he's strange?"

"He better not be too strange. My parents are in his hands."

"That's what happens when you grow old."

"How well do you know Kessinger?" I asked.

He gave this some thought, and then changed the subject.

"You've been seen gambling, you know."

"I make it no secret," I said.

"Well here's a secret. Get help."

"We all have our vices."

"But you have your vices with my money!"

Chapter 37

There was no choice except to head back to the track, since everybody knew where I was anyway. But I was thinking – I was thinking about Adolf and Kessinger. Was there a connection? Did Adolf have an interest in Kessinger's operation, a financial interest? His annual reports showed his fingers in every pot, including nursing homes, though none were mentioned by name. Now that was going too far. I was getting paranoid.

After I lost the first few races I didn't feel like playing anymore. I had to do something about the documentary that had plunged me in with Adolf. Not in a million years could I go through with it, but I would have to do something. The one and only solution was to pay him back his half a million, and the solution to that was the Kentucky Derby.

Then let him get Carlos Loomis to do the job. I could not stop every anti-Israel/anti-Semitic movie being made. So let it be Carlos Loomis. Not me. Never me.

I read all the latest news about the Derby and did something I never did – I read the summaries and opinions from the experts. Then I did something else. I went to the backstretch and starting having breakfast over there to do some scouting, and I met with trainers and jockeys and even the vet to find out if there was any special word. The horse I had picked out, for the time being, was Sensation. He was beautifully bred, came from a fine family, but his trainer was second rate.

His trainer had never won the Derby, and never had a horse for the Derby. Sensation would be his first shot. He'd be going off at relatively high odds. I had my hopes pinned on that horse, unless something better came along in the meantime. There was always a hot horse leading up to the Derby, or a "wise guy" horse. So far it wasn't Sensation.

The documentary I was working on was titled *Sinai*. I was going to follow the trek of the Israelites from Egypt to the Promised Land, and do it not religiously but scientifically, since no one was really sure which route they took, and no one even knew where Mount Sinai was, where Moses got the Ten Commandments. There were plenty of claims and counter-claims but no one really had his finger on the truth.

This had been my dream for some time. But I would have to make sure that it was scientific. I had already talked to a few people, archaeologists and doctors of divinity, and there was already some excitement afoot. There was no doubt, however, that religion would come into the picture. The first question was – did that event really happen? If so, are there any traces? Then, which sea did they actually cross?

When I wasn't studying the Bible for clues, I was studying the Racing Form for clues of a different kind.

Over at the backstretch, I had a talk with Javier Morena. He used to exercise horses for Sweeney, Sensation's trainer.

"Do you like him?" I asked about Sensation.

"Bowed tendons," he said, "but the horse has heart. Doesn't like to get beat."

I asked Doc Smith about bowed tendons. "Tendinitis shouldn't mean that much if treated properly," he said. "Quite common, the tear from the muscle to the bone."

I checked with a few more people and everybody had a different horse for the big race, a different horse and a different angle.

Falling in love with a horse was the same as falling in love with a woman. You never knew why.

Chapter 38

Barbara had me over for dinner. She'd been busy in the kitchen for days getting everything prepared.

"Are we celebrating something?" I asked.

She was severely overdressed.

"Are we expecting company?"

She laughed.

"Just you and me," she said. "We're the occasion."

She had music playing low, Sinatra.

She'd been to Florida to visit her sister and while there she'd made inquiries about nursing homes and found three perfect places in Boca Raton. One in particular she liked best, Sherrybrook Estates. She'd met the people who ran the place, was given the tour, and even took an unauthorized tour to find out how the residents really felt about the place, and it was all four stars.

"Nothing at all like Kessinger's," she said, "and you know we have to do something about this."

"Yes we do," I agreed.

"It's only getting worse."

"I feel the guilt every day."

"There is no guilt," she said. "Please. You did the best you could. We both did. We tried a hundred places before we arrived at that nuthouse. Who knew?"

But the cost was steep.

"Altogether," she said, "a bundle more than $200,000."

"A year?"

"No, but...well, very expensive."

"As if we're not paying a fortune already."

She said my mother had been calling her.

"Why not me?"

"Because you haven't been answering your phone, and because she didn't want to worry you."

"Go ahead."

"Your dad's been trying to starve himself."

"That can't be true," I said. "He's working on another novel."

"That's what I told your mother. Seems that he can't get anywhere with the novel. The words won't come. So he's given up altogether."

He was surely also worried about making it his Ninth novel.

"So he's not eating."

"She doesn't want to alert them about it because if she does, who knows? She's finally convinced, like your father, that they want to die you out."

"Doesn't sound like my mother."

"She's changed and I hate to tell you that, Gil. She's always been the level-headed one between the two, but..."

"I guess this means a trip to Florida."

"Maybe," she said, "some negotiating can be done about the price."

"Then there's the thousands I'll owe to break the contract with Kessinger."

"There is no easy answer. Otherwise how've you been?"

"Otherwise I've been okay and otherwise how've you been?"

"Missing you," she said.

I let that sit.

"You've lost weight."

"Can't be too rich or too thin," she said.

Not quite the story. Her sister had told me that she'd been losing weight worrying that we'd never get back together again. Her sister urged me to make a decision either way. Barbara was torn up about what she'd done, more than I could imagine, according to her sister, Florence. Take her back, or let her off the hook. She'd also been despairing about my *relationship* with Katrina. Was it serious? No, it was Hollywood.

My God! People were hurting everywhere!

I told Barbara about my plans for the Kentucky Derby.

"Oh! That could be thrilling," she said.

This much was true; she'd never been judgmental about my gambling.

"Can I go with you?" she asked.

I did have an extra seat, courtesy of Andre.

"We'll see," I said.

"I would love to go," she said. "Do you have a horse picked out?"

I told her that maybe I did, maybe I didn't.

"I remember your sitting there, doing your handicapping. I always found that so comforting."

She left to go to the kitchen and I thought I heard her sniffling.

"I'm sorry," she said when she came back. "I'm getting sentimental. I know you don't like people getting sentimental."

"Depends who, what, where, when."

"What do you mean by who?"

"Who is who."

We sat on this for a while.

"Does Katrina get sentimental over you?"

"Barbara..."

"Yes I am jealous, Gil, okay?"

Then: "Would you make love to me tonight?"

From across the table she gave me an unblinking stare that was almost disturbing for its icy determination.

"I'm asking, would you make love to me tonight, please."

"You know what Gore Vidal said."

"Yes," she said. "Never pass up a chance for sex or to appear on television. Well I'm not asking for television." Now she chuckled.

Somehow I knew it would come to this – this had been a set-up. The talk about another nursing home was genuine – but so was this.

"We had something, Gil."

Yes, I wanted to say, but then you went ahead and had something else.

"Yes we did," I said.

We were past the recriminations. That stage of it was done. What was it that author had said: sin, regret, retribution, atonement, forgiveness.

"Well I want it back," she said.

I had nothing to say or too much to say. Forgiveness was tough, a tough call, especially when it was about the woman you loved.

"But it doesn't have to be right away," she said. "We can take it slowly. But I need you to make love to me tonight."

"I don't operate well under pressure," I said.

She smiled. "Yes you do. Oh yes you do. With me you do."

I remembered that smile. When she got that way it was not easy resisting her.

"No promises, no commitments," she said.

Then: "Are the angels voting?"
"They haven't made up their minds," I said.
"Why don't you cast the deciding vote?"
I did.

Chapter 39

I was packing for a week's stay in Kentucky and had made reservations to visit some Blue Grass country. I had an invitation to stay at Blazing Rock Farms, one of the top breeding and training facilities in America and around the world. Blazing Rock had produced many true champions over the past 60 years. From there I'd move on to Churchill Downs in Louisville.

I had already done some advance wagering. I had put my money where my mouth was and risked $5,000 on Sensation for starters. This was when the urge took you over completely and you even forgot the wagering part, so strong was the nostalgia and the tradition and the romance of it all. All year, from track to track, the pull was for Kentucky and My Ol' Kentucky Home.

No World Series, no Super Bowl, no March Madness could compete with this, and it was one of the few times when the entire country came together as a family.

But first I had to do something dangerous.

I joined Barbara for a quick trip to visit and check out Sherrybrook Estates in Boca Raton. I was introduced to Mac McDonald who ran the place, along with his wife, Kathleen. They seemed foursquare. He was a Vietnam vet, which right away made him legit. He invited me to his home. We shared a love of baseball and incredibly, horseracing, though he was a two-dollar bettor. I tested

him, and he knew horses. I liked everything he said –
that no nursing home (and he hated the term) could
ever be perfect, for obvious reasons, but that at the very
least, the "guests" should not be forgotten, neglected and
abandoned.

Most important, the "guests" must be shown that life
goes on, and for that purpose a nursery school was situated directly next door.

"Now our elderly have daily contact with children. We
have visitations back and forth, and I assure you that it
adds years to the aged."

"The children love it, too," said Kathleen.

I was sold, but they could not come down on the price.

On the plane ride back Barbara was high on life, especially after a few drinks. She was quite giddy.

"Oh God," she said. "Just think..."

"Unfortunately that's what I'm doing."

"The money," she said.

"Yes, the money," I said.

"We'll have to find a way," she said.

She was back to saying *we* after her triumphant se-
duction. Everything went well; quite fantastic, really.

Barbara had not forgotten her tricks. She knew how
to bring out the best in me – or was it the worst? She
liked her sex raunchy and dirty and I complied. There
was a time, not so long ago, in a hotel room, when her
shouts drew the police, who left saluting me in admira-
tion. This time only the walls of her apartment muffled
her shrieks. Of all the women, there was still only
Barbara.

"You'll find a way," she said, snuggling up.

Yes I would find a way. But there was trouble ahead.
Dear Lord, there is trouble ahead.

The angels were voting again, but this time would it be to the devil to cast the deciding ballot?

"You always do," she said.

I do? I could not remember the last time I made the right decision, about anything. It hit me that every decision I had ever made was the wrong decision – though here again we go to the races for the metaphor of life. The lesson there is to always go with your instinct; never second-guess your first choice. How many times had I kicked myself for outsmarting myself, for thinking too much when the winner was right there in my hands? Too much wisdom leads to folly.

Too often I'd switched choices at the last second and paid for it in heartbreak. There were no *second instincts.* All along you really had but one choice to get it right.

Earlier she had handed me a gift and insisted that I not open it until we got on the plane, and so I opened it, and it was (perhaps?) a first edition of F. Scott Fitzgerald's *The Crack-Up* – his finest work, we both agreed – and in it she had inscribed: "Finally he was wrong. There *are* second acts in American lives. There *are* second chances, if only we'd open our eyes."

She nudged me with naughty eyes.

"We never tried this, did we?" she said glancing downward where all depravity begins.

"You're thinking what I'm thinking," I said.

"Aha."

True, we had never tried the Mile High Club.

"You don't mean the bathroom," I said.

"No I don't," she whispered.

This would be awkward, right here at our seats. But the lights were out and most of our fellow passengers were asleep.

"First this," she said.

That was the easy part. I slid my hand underneath her sweater and grabbed a handful. She'd been wearing no bra, or had taken it off in the bathroom earlier. There was quite a handful to take and her nipples had grown hard. Then I slid my hand down, down and down, and she was wearing no panties, either, and I worked her there until she began to moan, and I kept working there until she began to moan louder. I was afraid she'd get too loud but when she unzipped me and started stroking me I stopped caring about anything else. The next part would be the tricky part, but we had a blanket and we covered ourselves with it, and using contortions impossible for the human body, I got on top of her, inserted, and worked her to a near climax, and neither of us cared if we were being seen or heard, and then she got on top of me, slightly sideways, and pumping madly, got herself to climax fully; and only then did she go to the bathroom to return with a wet tissue to clean me there, and then, still covered, she got to her knees, and finished me off as well.

She did not return from this drowsiness as she usually did. She was in high spirits.

"Oh I needed that," she declared. "Does it ever hit you like it hits me?"

"Sometimes," I had to admit, but I did not admit that it only hits me when I think of her; Barbara, only Barbara.

"I get so horny," she said, "but only for you."

Was this how married people talk, or was this how separated people talk?

"I think good days are coming," she said, kissing me. "Don't you think?"

I wasn't so sure.

If she saw the brightness, I saw the darkness. My mind was working on all the possibilities, on all that could go wrong and there was so much that could go wrong. There was so much that could turn out badly no matter which path I took. Danger ahead, nothing but danger, that was all I saw. This or that – there would be a price. But I would not spoil it for her, by telling her what I was really thinking. Let her have this moment.

Back at her apartment she had made plans for me to stay over. She had on Max Bruch's Scottish Fantasy, which she knew always sucked me in.

But I had other plans.

There were troubles ahead. Dear Lord, there is trouble ahead.

Chapter 40

Now there were only days to go before the Derby when I would risk everything on an all or nothing bid to save everything that needed saving. But I could not wait that long, not even that long. So I went to the casino to see if I could get a lucky day, even though I knew that there were no such things, no lucky days, no lucky hours, no lucky signs. All that was superstition and so heathen.

I went to the casino and played practically all the table games just to see if I could get hot, and yes, I did make out at the dice. I found the hot shooter and when the dice came round to me I had a hot hand and started hitting my points, no cursed seven showing up. Soon the table got crowded. Word got around. Word gets around. The crowding and the noise and the hollering from the boys to keep it going caused me the sort of stress and anxiety that sometimes led to my dizzy spells and even those blinding headaches.

So I was unsteady on my feet and I had to keep one hand on the table for support; the stickman warning me to keep hands off, but I was worried. I was near to passing out, and I knew it was bad, that I was in bad shape, when, in an instant, I saw no faces and heard no noise. Everything was empty and dark. I kept shooting automatically. The dice flew out of my hand from memory.

Finally I sevened-out, but did not know it; I asked for them back, surprising the stickman who said something, something about being done.

"New shooter," he said, and that I did hear.

I said no, it's still my turn, and I kept waiting for the dice to be handed back to me.

"New shooter," said the pit boss.

No, I said, the dice belong to me.

Some of the boys laughed and some of the boys said, yes, give him back those ivories.

"You sevened-out," said the stickman in a reasonable tone.

"Not me," I said.

I thought I saw the pit boss get on the phone.

"It's all rigged," I said.

"Sir."

Someone was tapping me on the shoulder

I saw a man in uniform, but blurred as I was to my surroundings, I didn't recognize the uniform.

"What country is this?" I said.

"Sir, please leave the table."

"What country are you from?" I said. "Who's taken over?"

"Sir, please."

"It's all rigged, you know."

"Sir, one more time."

"Nobody gets a break."

"Okay," and as I was being led away I found myself quoting that man who said, *Each man is in it alone and should expect no favors.*

That's what I kept saying; "Each man is in it alone and should expect no favors."

I was not taken into Security. I was taken into the casino's Medical Center. A nurse took my pulse and asked me the day of the week – the month, the year.

Apparently I was giving the right answers, but still, she said I should get myself looked after.

A doctor came over. He made all the usual checks.

"You cracked up out there," he laughed.

He said that this sort of reaction was not altogether unusual.

"We see everything in this setting," he said.

He said that he had checked me out on Google and discovered that I was no lunatic but even somewhat famous.

He especially liked my documentary on the cruelty of forced female circumcision.

"We actually saw your film as part of a class," he said.

He calmed me down, and I was beginning to feel better.

"You think you can get back out there to the civilized world?" he said with a friendly and knowing chuckle.

I said I would try to behave.

I went to the bathroom to wash up and to steady myself. I was a big winner, but not big enough.

I played some machines, which I seldom did, never did when I was in control, but maybe this was my day after all, and got one machine that was talking to me. I kept getting dealt solid hands and when that game got cold, I switched to the Keno. I played four spots at the maximum dollar amount and hit a minor jackpot, but still I felt unsteady and still I felt no thrill.

When that got cold I moved over to the high limit poker parlor and there I put back some of my winnings, and there a woman complained about my smoking.

I alerted her to the sign that said *Smoking Permitted in this Section*, but she stormed off, leaving me with a curse.

This I did not need. Now we believe in curses? Who are these people and who sends these people?

I decided that this was enough and went to the restaurant for my usual soup and salad. I needed a friendly face, and it was the waitress Susan.

"I've been out sick," she said.

"Oh, I'm sorry."

"You've probably been asking for me," she said.

"Yes I have," I said, which was not the truth.

The truth was that people came and went and for you, one server was as good as another, and for them, one gambler was the same as another.

We were replaceable parts. We were non-essential personnel.

Then I went to the races.

"You still going with your big horse?" asked Andre.

"Sensation," I said. "Yes, Sensation."

"I hear he's got sore legs."

"They all do," I said. "They run a thousand pounds on toothpicks."

"What the hell was going on out there?" asked Andre.

"People," I said.

"You made quite a scene."

"They took my dice," I said.

"Hey, Gil."

"What?"

"Are we starting to lose you, man?"

"I'm okay."

"Not from what I saw."

"That's open to interpretation."

"They could have arrested you, my friend, and you do know that you had sevened-out. Please tell me you know that, please."

"I guess," I said. "I guess so."

"Just checking. We don't want to lose a man like you."

"But it is rigged, you know."

"That's what I keep telling you. Nobody gets a fair shake. I've been telling you that from the start. Why don't you go home?"

"This *is* home," I said.

"Hah!"

Jay Garfield wasn't there but he was on the line.

"News travels fast," I said after he asked me if I was okay.

"From what I hear you broke down in mid-stretch," he said.

"Minor misunderstanding, surely all my fault."

"Piling up on you, is it?" he asked.

"What about you?"

He said he was happy. His trainer's license hadn't come in yet, so he was walking horses for Doc Rivers.

Jay Garfield, once master of the journalistic universe, now a hotwalker.

O How the Mighty Have Fallen.

Chapter 41

"You do know the walls have ears," Adolf Gruberman was saying. "There's more than the eye in the sky. There's the ear in the sky."

I needed this lecture?

I knew well the Wisdom of the Fathers; *An eye sees, an ear hears, and everything is recorded in a Book.*

Right, there were no secrets.

"So what your friend Jay Garfield said to you, it has been heard," said Adolf.

"And reported, I suppose."

Adolf was just warming up. "So he says about me that I don't kill with bullets, right?"

"I don't remember."

"He says I don't kill with bullets, I kill with ink. Now do you remember?"

"No I do not remember."

"Let me refresh, or let me put it like this – DO NOT BE TOO SURE."

There had been rumors that some men who had displeased him, gone, suddenly disappeared. So it was never only about the ink.

"You're threatening me?"

"Advising you. Be careful."

Apparently his darling daughter had found someone.

I had taken a chance and asked him for more money. That's the fix I was in. I needed the money for Boca Raton, to get my parents out there quick. The cost would be heavy. First I'd have to pay Kessinger his $70,000 for breaking the contract, and then pay a huge sum to the McDonalds. There wasn't much choice. This was a panic move, but I had no choice, and all things considered, I would have to make that movie of his after all.

Yet how could I make that film...and yet how could I leave Mom and Dad where they were...they were in Sodom all right. So I had to make the film.

They were in a place where *each man was on his own and should expect no favors.*

"Give me the film and I will give you the money, and if you don't give me the film, I cannot be responsible what happens to you. Other people are involved."

Other people.

"I have to answer to people as well as you do," Adolf was saying. "I have to deliver them a movie, as promised, or...or I have to deliver YOU."

Chapter 42

My big chance, my only chance was the Kentucky Derby. The odds against winning big, really big, were not favorable. But it had to be tried.

If I made that film, that would kill my father slowly. My God, his name associated with smut, political porn!

But if I didn't make the film, he would surely die, along with Mom. There was no future at Kessinger's. There was only death and despair.

So it came down to this after all. To save my mom and dad I'd have to darken my name with a work that was sure to cut me off from my people.

How does one do this?

I had everything ready to go, and I was confident in my handicapping. Gambling had gotten me into much of this, and gambling would have to get me out. Let it be so. I am compulsive, a compulsive gambler. Okay. But if in the past it was wasteful and sinful, all this gambling, this time it was for a *mitzvah*, a good deed. Shouldn't the angels vote in my favor, if only just this once?

I drove to the airport and kept my phone dark. I wanted no calls, no messages, no interference.

I kept turning this over in my mind; to save my parents I'd have to make an anti-Semitic film. Or pay off Gruberman.

So this was a good deed I was doing. Yes, gambling can be for the greater good.

At the airport, I decided to relent. The message was from Barbara, that I was to turn back right away.

Chapter 43

My father had died taking a walk outside his bungalow. A man told me this before I got into the house.

He said, "Are you his son?"

"Yes."

"He fell over and nobody helped him up. Don't tell anybody I told you or I'm a dead man myself."

I went in and Barbara was consoling Mom.

"He didn't want to go on," Mom said.

I did not mention what I'd just heard. That would be no help.

Mom's grieving worried me. She'd always been the strong one, but she'd always needed her strength for one man, and that man was gone.

I wept, and Barbara let it be. She had already done her weeping. She loved my dad as he had loved her.

He had to be buried right away, according to Jewish tradition. But Kessinger stepped in with other ideas. He said he had a wonderful memorial service all planned out, including his own personal eulogy. This was to take place in four days. I said no, today. He said no, four days.

"We have our own customs," he said.

"We have our own traditions," I said.

"I am sorry," he said. "But you should have read the contract. Funeral services and funerals take place on our premises. It's in the contract."

I asked where in the contract it says that when a man falls down, no one is to help him back up?

"Who told you this?"

Of course I refused.

"We'll find out," he said.

"I will also find out and I will sue."

"Sir, I can't blame you for being upset..."

"My father is being buried at King David Cemetery, in the morning. Do not try to stop this. I warn you."

He knew what I was talking about when I added, "I intend to call for an investigation of this place, and I will make a movie of this investigation."

He slammed the door behind him and my father was buried the next morning at King David Cemetery.

Chapter 44

We brought Mom over to my apartment, and more than that, Barbara moved in as well.

Mom showed me a letter Dad had written for my eyes only: "God forgives. Why can't you?"

So I did. I simply did. I forgave the woman that I loved because I loved her.

Chapter 45

I went over to see Adolf Gruberman.

"I'll have the movie ready for you in a month."

He wrote me a check for $250,000.

That was a three-quarter of a million dollar movie that I owed him.

Chapter 46

Barbara and I drove Mom to Boca Raton. She refused to fly. I paid the McDonalds $200,000.

We promised we'd come visit often.

Mom wept.

"I'm so happy to see you both together again. Dad wanted this so badly."

Chapter 47

The footage I had assembled for Adolf Gruberman's movie – I burned every inch into ashes.

He has turned to Carlos Loomis to start from scratch.

He has not yet turned his attention to me.

I wait. I'm a gambler.